The Clutching Hands

"Is Adams your lover?" he asked.

"Of course he is," she answered angrily.

Suddenly, he grabbed her by the shoulder. And just as suddenly, his hands encircled her throat. She wanted to scream but sound came out in a whisper. She tried to pry his hands loose but they held like a vise.

The anger was gone now. In its place was fear and an overwhelming need to breathe. But the gripping hands would not allow it.

The world was a redness dimming around her. She cried out once more. Then there was silence . . . the silence of death.

This is the fast-paced story of a beautiful girl who had one lover too many.

William Holder

The Case of the DEAD DIVORCEE

N·A·L SIGNET BOOKS

A SIGNET BOOK

Published by THE NEW AMERICAN LIBRARY

FIRST PRINTING, JUNE, 1958

SIGNET BOOKS are published by
The New American Library of World Literature, Inc.
501 Madison Avenue, New York 22, New York

PRINTED IN THE UNITED STATES OF AMERICA

Prologue

SHE AWAKENED UNWILLINGLY and unconsciously felt for the form beside her, then realized she was alone. She lay for a moment almost entirely unaware, then remembering slowly she stretched and smiled. She turned and sought sleep again and was suddenly alive to a repetition of the knock on the door that had aroused her. She reached out an arm and turned on the bed-table light. The small clock told her it was a quarter to five. He had been gone less than an hour. He wouldn't come back at this time. Or would he? It was an interesting thought. His return might lead to a decision neither of them had thought it necessary to make. The knock on the door echoed through the apartment again.

She got up quickly, her body recoiling from the coolness of the room after the warm bed. She put on a woolen robe and mules, ran a comb through her hair at the dressing table. She went into the living room, lighting a lamp, and at the door said, "Who is it?"

A voice she knew, but not the one she had thought to hear said, "Ann, I want to see you. It's important."

She hesitated for only a moment, fighting back the disappointment she felt, then she opened the door. "It's a fine time to come calling."

The man came into the room, and she closed the door and looked at him. He had been drinking, of course. It was hardly unusual. "Do you know that it's a quarter to five?"

"I didn't think you'd mind. After all, one visitor just left."

Anger flooded her. "What have you been doing, standing out on the street spying on me?" The goodness of the night had turned into a bitter, sick thing.

The man said, "What was he doing up here until this hour?"

"What business is it of yours? You have nothing to do with me!"

"I love you. You know that. And that gives me the right. . . ."

She stared at him for a moment, then laughed at him. "You love me? *You?* You must be out of your mind."

She turned away from him but he caught at her shoulder. When she looked at his face she first became aware of her danger. She did not move.

"It's been going on for quite some time, hasn't it?" the man said. "He has a home away from home. Very cozy."

She said nothing. She tried to move away but the hand on her shoulder was strong and detained her.

"I'm surprised at you," he said. "Carrying on such a business in a nice respectable town like this. Don't you think they know?" He moved his head in a gesture that included the sleeping village. "Don't you think they talk about you?"

"Take your hand off me," she said. She could feel the tremor of whatever passion held him. "Get out of here."

He shook his head. "Not until you tell me what I want to know. He's your lover, isn't he?"

"Get out of here," she said again. "What I do is entirely my own business."

"Not when someone loves you, it isn't. Didn't you know that? Is he your lover? You might as well tell me, since what I think doesn't seem to make much difference to you."

The anger was in her again, and a pride. "Of course he is," she said. "Whatever else did you think?"

The hand snapped from her shoulder to her throat and was joined by the other. She tried to scream but the effort was stifled in her throat and emerged as a sort of whine. She tore at the hands but they were vises. She screamed, *This can't be happening! Not to me!* But the words were merely a pressure building up in the back of her eyes. She stared at the face before her and tried desperately to claw at it but the long arms held her off. Fear was gone and anger, now, and the only important thing was to breathe but the gripping hands would not allow it. She strained impossibly and the world was a redness dimming around her. She cried out once again silently.

Chapter 1

As Adams and Tate reached the sidewalk they encountered the first of the reporters. There were three men and a photographer. The camera was used quickly and often, but Tate brushed aside the queries. "No comment. You'll get all the story you want inside, if I know Sands." He told Adams, "Better develop a manner. You'll see plenty of them from now on."

When they were in the car, Adams said, "I must say I've been in more comfortable situations."

"They'd be easy to find."

"It really looks rough?"

The lawyer said, "Before I answer that, there are a few things I'll have to know. How well did you know Ann Durant?"

"Very well."

"We won't go into that any further at the moment. How long had you known her?"

"A couple of months, more or less."

"Were you in her apartment the night before last?"

"Yes."

"What time did you leave?"

Adams thought about that. "It was pretty close to four o'clock yesterday morning."

"That's about the time they have pegged for the murder."

Adams didn't answer.

"It's my understanding that you're married."

"That's right."

"Well, in answer to your question of a few moments ago: It really looks rough." Tate drove silently for a few seconds. "Those men we just left are not fools. A murder was committed and it's their job to find out who did it. They are going to ask questions and they're going to come up with answers."

"They asked plenty last night."

"They haven't started yet. Their very stubborn inquiries are going to place you in Ann Durant's apartment at four o'clock in the morning. Evidently Mrs. Greer and Alice Stanton saw you on the streets at that time and it stands to reason you weren't looking at the moon."

"I don't like it that much."

Tate persisted. "They are going to find out whether or not you and Ann Durant were lovers. They are going to find out what your grades were in grammar school and if you were ever fined for spitting on the sidewalk. If you ever got angry enough to curse at your wife, they are going to know it."

Adams tried to fight off the depression that was enveloping him. "I've been known to say 'hell' and 'damn'."

"They are going to come up with a very solid motive for the murder," Tate said. He paused for several seconds. "I could supply them with one right now. Ann Durant wanted you to marry her. She was going to your wife and tell her that you and Durant were in love and you wanted a divorce. You regarded your affair with her as just a casual thing and didn't want your marriage disrupted. You quarreled with her and strangled her in a fury."

"That's pretty hypothetical," Adams said, but Tate's words frightened him.

"The way they'll present it to a jury of twelve average people in a few months might not seem so hypothetical."

"A jury," Adams said. His thinking on the matter hadn't progressed that far.

"We'll have to talk a lot more about this, of course, but right from here it looks like an open-and-shut case with you as the bookmark. What do you know about her friends? Or her enemies."

Adams reflected that he knew very little about either. Then he remembered what he should never have forgotten at all. "Her former husband is staying at Bald Mountain. She saw him a few days ago."

Tate whistled softly. "That could be good or it could be very bad. It supplies you with another motive. They were going to reconcile, you couldn't stand the thought and killed her."

Adams nodded almost absently. Then he said, "Or he might have heard she was seeing me and killed her himself."

"How long had they been divorced?"

"A couple of years."

"That's not very long. Feelings persist."

That was something Adams could agree to. "She said he was the possessive type. Didn't like to lose anything he'd once owned." He wondered if there was a hint of desperation in his voice.

Tate drove silently for a few moments. "I don't think anything will happen for a week or so. Mr. District Attorney Sands is going to be very thorough. He's publicity crazy and he likes this one. It's going to grow a lot of headlines. BEAUTIFUL DIVORCEE KILLED IN LOVE NEST. Things like that."

Adams cringed. Almost from the first he had envisioned what was going to happen. "That's great. How do we stop that?"

"It would be as impossible as stopping an avalanche. You are in this up to your ears. You'll stay in it until we can get you out. If we can get you out."

"You're full of good cheer."

"I'm a lawyer, not a comedian. You're jammed up. The more Sands examines this the more certain he's going to be that he has a sure thing. He'll probably ask for increased bail in a day or two."

"I imagine we can take care of that," Adams said.

Tate glanced at him. "You're not thinking of running."

Adams shook his head. "What good could that do me?"

"Very little. You don't run far, these days."

When had there ever been a place to run to? Adams thought.

"What we might do is hire a couple of detectives to do a little investigating for us." Tate turned. "Do you think there might have been another man involved? Currently, I mean?"

Adams said, "No," without hesitation.

"I didn't mean to be insulting. We have to explore every possibility. We'll have to look into Mrs. Durant's background; any enemies she might have had around here, any in the past. The husband, of course, should be gone over thoroughly. Although I imagine the police will be asking him a few questions."

"I don't think they have many left," Adams said, thinking of the night he had spent.

"Were they tough with you last night?"

Adams considered the question. The hours had been

countless, the exhaustion complete. "Insistent, let's say."

Tate nodded. "They can be. And there'll be more of it. They can haul you in for questioning at any time."

"That's a pleasant thought."

"None of this is pleasant."

In a moment Adams said, "They didn't give me any of the . . . details." He remembered how he had left her.

"She was lying on the living-room floor. She was wearing only a robe. Nothing had been disturbed and there was no sign of a forced entry."

Adams nodded. "What do I tell the police when they do this repeated hauling in business?"

"Actually, you don't have to open your mouth. That way they learn nothing."

"I understand they can be persuasive."

Tate shook his head. "Not on anything like this. They wouldn't dare."

"Well, that's nice. So I say absolutely nothing?"

Tate said, "The attitude has its drawbacks. It puts you in a very guilty light and the less co-operative you are the more insistent they are going to be. Look, suppose you have dinner with me and we go over everything we can think of. Then you'll be at least slightly prepared to deal with Sands and his merry men."

Adams nodded. "Good. Except that you have dinner with me."

"Whatever you say." They were driving into West Fork. "I imagine you'll want to go right up to your place?"

"Thanks, but don't bother. Drop me at Cooley's. I think I could stand a drink just about now. Thank you for everything."

Tate's expression sobered. "There's another thing. I made inquiries. They performed an autopsy and found out all they could, and Mrs. Durant's brother is arriving this evening to take the body home. Ohio, I think it is."

The body. The last trip, and farewell had already been said. Adams said, "All right. Thank you."

They stopped in front of Cooley's and Tate said, "Around seven, John?"

"Seven is fine, Bill," Adams said, and only when the car had driven away did he become aware of the use of first names. It had been unconscious with him, as it must have been with Tate. It pleased him. He could use a few friends just about now.

It was eleven thirty when he went into The Tavern and sat at a table near the bar, tired to the bone, and thought of the events of the last few days. Murderous events. There was no waking out of this nightmare. It stayed with you.

Joe Cooley came out of the kitchen and approached the table. He said, "Hello, Johnny. A hell of a mess."

Adams nodded. "I was just sitting here wondering how I ever got into it." But he remembered, all right. It seemed years ago.

Chapter 2

THE FRENZY OF THE ALARM CLOCK brought Adams close to a state approaching consciousness, and his groping hand shut off the clangor. He got out of the twin bed with all the grace of a mechanical man and found his way from bedroom to bathroom through some atavistic hunting instinct. He somehow arranged the shower so that he was not immediately scalded to death, and once the locked steel hinges had been melted from his elbows, knees and back, he turned on the cold. A half minute of this brought him fully alive and he took another ten seconds of punishment for insurance. He shaved, brushed his teeth, found fresh linen, socks, slacks and shoes, and went through the bedroom and the huge living room to the kitchen. He was still in a slight daze as he made two very solid whisky sours on the rocks. It had been a long evening, he remembered vaguely, and he cursed himself for having called an eight o'clock rehearsal for this morning.

He turned at the sound of a door opening and said, "Good morning, Mamie."

Mamie Doyle, emerging from her room off the kitchen, was a spare woman in her middle fifties. Her face was triangular, her eyes observant and usually noncommittal, her mouth generous, her gray hair neatly arranged. She shook her head. "Those nasty, lemony things so early in the morning will be the death of you and the girl." Her years of association with the Adamses had given her conversational privileges she would have assumed anyway.

"Mamie, they're the miracle drink, the great restorative."

"Doyle always liked beer after a brannigan. Soothing, he said it was."

"He was right, but I haven't got time to be soothing myself. All I hope for is to come partly alive. I've got to be at the studio at eight o'clock."

She glanced at the wall clock. "Then you'll have time for a proper breakfast. What would you like?"

He winced at the thought of food. "Black coffee. Toast." He took the sours and retraced his path to the bedroom.

His wife Helen was somehow awake, sitting up in bed smoking a cigarette. Ordinarily lovely, with her striking features, stunning figure and flaming red hair, she was in some way not at her best this morning. He put one of the glasses on the table at her side, raised his own in silent salute and tasted it. He blessed the sainted man who had invented the drink.

Helen said, "I heard the alarm and remembered that I have to be in early too. We stayed much too late. I must look a fright."

"The usual repair job should take care of everything."

Her lovely mouth tightened. "Hardly a flattering thing to say to a woman."

"It's just that we were up late and we weren't sipping milk. No offense." After six years and the way things had been going lately, he was losing a touch of his gallantry. "You're a gay morning sprite," he tried. "Dew-touched."

"Scotch-dipped," she amended. "Let it go."

Let it go. The phrase could apply to their relationship, at this stage. The quarrels and the prolonged periods of not speaking were becoming more frequent. He had an idea of just about where the unrest had started and he did not want it to continue but he did not know exactly what to do about it. He said things he did not want to say, did things he had no appetite for, out of anger and frustration and sometimes out of what he recognized as a mistaken sense of pride. What did a couple of people do, he wondered, when their marriage was all broken up and neither wanted to admit it? Where did the pieces go, so that perhaps you could find them and patch them together again?

Helen tasted her drink, then took a long swallow. "I guess we shouldn't have gone to the Rileys'."

"But we had to limp along because, as you said, *everyone* in television would be there. That was sufficient reason for not going."

"You have to face up to affairs like that, Johnny. You know that? If only to keep the knives out of your back."

"My back looks like a punchboard. It's becoming unimportant to me. Did I tell you about the stinking show they've got for me this week?"

"You mentioned something about a little boy and a dog."

Adams nodded grimly. "And his estranged parents who become reconciled when the little boy is hurt and the dog goes and gets both of them—separately, mind you—and tugs them to the hospital bedside."

"It's Americana," Helen grinned at him evilly. "Good, meaty stuff for a man the critics have named one of the best producer-writer-directors in TV."

Adams drank. "What's the use? They killed 'Offbeat' after four shows, before it had a chance." He had used young actors, young writers with fresh ideas. He'd succeeded in making his point without the use of a six-inch paint brush. Three of the shows had been really good. He'd gotten laughs and he'd brought that big lump up in the throat of the audience. But the sponsor hadn't liked what he'd seen. "It's highbrow stuff," he'd said. "My wife doesn't understand it at all. Who cares about a shoe clerk if he's homely?"

Adams came back to the present. "And how goes 'Helen's Household Hints'? I haven't tuned in on it lately." Helen had a show that ran for fifteen minutes each weekday afternoon on which she divested cookery of most of its witchlike aspects. Simplicity was the secret, Helen smilingly insisted each day. No need to be frightened by awesome recipes. Take the preposterous prescription firmly in hand, stare it in the eye and almost before you have time to doff the frilly apron and show the stunning dinner gown to full advantage, the table is laden with a gustatory masterpiece that looks as if it had been assembled by a group of cunning pixies.

The only catch was that Helen had difficulty boiling water. It was her beauty, her figure that flattered clothes, her thoroughly phony and assured manner, that kept her on the air. Those attributes, and Mamie Doyle's amazing culinary artistry, the surface characteristics of which she readily imparted to Helen.

"It's boring me to death," Helen said. "How enthusiastic can you get about ruffled tripe, or whatever you do to it?"

"You might learn to cook it. If Mamie had a swooning fit or something we'd starve."

"Mamie was made in heaven, but I don't think she can wear an evening gown as well as I."

"There are certain points of difference between you," Adams admitted. "At the moment she's determined that I eat something. I'll have to try to please her."

He was almost to the door when Helen said, "You seemed to be paying a lot of attention to Sue Crane last night. It was rather noticeable."

Adams thought about that. "Couple of things might have influenced me. She's pretty and she talks well. And she didn't have Harry Blake hanging around her neck." He went into the kitchen thinking about Blake. He'd been doing a lot of that, lately.

In silence he had coffee, toast and scrambled eggs. He thought of the work that was going badly, of the marriage that was somehow weakening. He was unaware that his discomfort was so evident until Mamie Doyle said,

"Is it the job that's bothering you?" He was about to make some noncommittal answer when she asked, "Or is it the girl?"

He tried to pass it off. "That girl happens to be twenty-nine years old."

"And it's time she had some children, she and you."

"We had one," Adams said. "For almost six months. Remember?" He recalled easily the joy and the pride, and he would never forget the shocking emptiness the pneumonia had brought into their lives. There had been the table-pounding grief, the self-recriminations; and above all, the void that could not be filled.

"I'll not forget," the gray woman said. "But I've seen families with more than one child. You're both young and strong."

"But maybe not that tough," Adams said. The thought of enduring such an episode again horrified him, and the fear in Helen of a recurrence of their tragedy was too strong for him to contest.

"It wouldn't happen again," Mamie said.

"I guess you're right there," Adams said. "It won't." He got himself a tie and jacket, told his wife he'd see her later, and went out into the cool of the early October morning.

Chapter 3

IT WAS USUALLY a pleasant half-hour walk to the studio, but his thoughts were not amiable this morning. He sorted them out and settled on Harry Blake. Blake worked for Barlow-Madden, an advertising agency handling three of their largest accounts. One of these was the sponsor of Adams' current show, "This Evening." Blake was large, lean and handsome and possessed an off-hand charm Adams sensed to be coldly calculated. He was a man with an eye for the agency's splendid dollar and although Adams conceded this to be a reasonable attitude, he felt that Blake's more-than-ordinary concern with the minutiae of each presentation was unwarranted. During the last year he'd been under the strong impression it had been more than coincidental that any program he produced for a Blake account had met with more major changes and minor annoyances than had been his usual experience.

The man's attitude toward Helen, while obvious, did not lend itself to any strenuous objection. They frequently, in the course of their work, socialized with loosely the same people. Blake was always attentive to Helen in a company of people, but always correct. In a company of people. Adams had no idea whether or not they saw each other privately but was under no illusions that it was an impossibility.

Since the death of the baby two years ago things had been going downhill, if almost imperceptibly. He had heard of deep sorrow acting as a unifying, strengthening force, but somehow such had not been the case in their misfortune, and Adams felt himself to blame in this. He'd been selfish with his grief and had sought to squander it in vast expenditures of energy. He had buried himself in work, not to the point of total disregard of Helen's prostration, it was true, but there had been many hours he might have spent with her in attempting to alleviate her misery instead of concentrating on the disbursement of his own. Perhaps that had been the point of the wedge that had separated them. Granting that Helen was an emotionally disturbed woman and Blake an attractive and proximate man, where did that leave him?

But then if it weren't Blake it might well be someone else. People were not meant to live in loneliness, and that was what he and Helen were doing now, even though they shared the same home. The fine sympathies that had welded them were rusted and decaying and he could think of no effective restoratives. Or perhaps he didn't want to. He wasn't sure. It might be that they had played out their particular string and the game was ended. They had known great happiness and they had suffered their tragedy, and maybe the cycle was completed.

At the studio he had no time to ponder the problem. What yesterday he had thought he'd beaten into a sneering semblance of order was once more unrelieved chaos. The dog's supposed master had obviously spent the night in high wassail and his demented cur seized upon this fine opportunity to ignore every hiccuped command. The child star of the masterpiece, an utterly untalented little monster with the unlikely name of Westmore Warwick, had the sulks. He refused to do the hospital near-deathbed scene unless he were permitted to wear his outer-space helmet. After an interminable delay his mother convinced him of his earthliness by warming his plump bottom.

Then, just about when everything had been straightened out to the point where Adams was hopeful of retaining his sanity for another day or two, Blake interrupted the rehearsal. Adams looked upon the easy, apologetic smile, listened to the even, sympathetic voice, and decided he was not half thrilled to death.

"Johnny," Blake said, "I know this might cause you a little inconvenience and I wouldn't trouble you for the world at this point, but it's from—you know."

"Give me three guesses. The sponsor, or the sponsor, or the sponsor."

Blake nodded. "He feels that instead of having a little boy in the part, we should use a little girl. You know, cute as hell with curls and pretty dresses and all that. More appeal, more tears."

Adams nodded. "Frankly, I agree with you. It would

save the whole stinking production if we could get hold of Marilyn Monroe." Then he said, "Blake, are you out of your mind? Do you know that this horror goes on tomorrow night? The whole thing would have to be redone and we'd have to find another little genius to play the part. Aside from the fact that this thing was written—you'll pardon the expression—with the idea in mind that little *boys* had dogs. Little girls have dolls, remember?"

Blake made an apologetic gesture. "I know it would be a little trouble, Johnny, but after all . . ."

"I'd have to give it a great deal of thought," Adams said. He covered his eyes with his hand for a split second, then lowered it. "No."

Blake's mind was so filled with understanding he had to shake his head to clear it. "I know exactly how you feel, Johnny. But if you take that attitude, I'm afraid I'll have to see B.J."

'B.J.,' a very stuffy character named Applegate, was vice president in charge of the Barlow-Madden account. Adams tapped Blake lightly on the chest. "You do that. And give Applegate my best. My very best." He returned to his impossible task.

He broke the rehearsal for lunch and went for a short walk, too distracted to eat. That the show would be presented to a nation-wide audience in slightly more than twenty-four hours was utterly unthinkable, yet he knew it would be done. By some miracle, the details of which continued to elude him even after years of witnessing it, the program would start on schedule, the cast would perform its onerous duties in an acceptable fashion, and exactly one half hour after the mess had started it would finish, right on time and milked dry. But it was a miracle in which even a devotee could have no fore-faith. You had to be there, help it occur, and only when those last agonizing seconds had run through the clock and you were off the air could you believe it.

He went back to the studio, knocked his brains out for another torturous two hours, then dismissed the company until the final rehearsal on the morrow. Drained of strength and of hope, he slumped in a chair and sought renewal in a cigarette. He turned on a studio set and watched his wife triumph casually over a cheese soufflé she would not have approached the making of with a ten-foot pole in her own kitchen. The fact that the end product, appetizingly portrayed, had been constructed by Mamie two hours before and treated by her in some mystic manner that lent it the appearance of immediacy, detracted nothing from Helen's loveliness. She was, he decided as he saw her smilingly and offhandedly deal with ingredients she loathed as she did snakes, one of the world's great actresses.

Back in the closet that was laughingly referred to as his office, there was a memo urging him to call Mr. Applegate. This he did.

"John," said Applegate, "I understand you refuse to consider a very clever suggestion made by our sponsor."

"Yes and no. I refuse to consider the suggestion. It was not clever."

"That's an extremely valuable account, John."

"It's unusual, too. It represents an instance where a successful business is apparently run by a moron."

There was an ominous silence on the other end of the wire. "Your attitude is hardly co-operative, John. I'm afraid I'll have to consult with Mr. G. about this."

In his attempts to resolve the complicated gradings of the system's hierarchy, Adams had concluded that Phillip Gordon seemed to be top man. You could never be sure, of course, but at least it seemed that way. "Good," Adams said. "Give him my love." He hung up.

Mark Hall, who assisted him, came into the cubicle and sat on the edge of the desk. He said, "Nothing will convince me that both the dog and that horrible small child aren't high in the pay of the rival network."

Adams made one of his more brilliant observations. "A drink would do neither of us a great deal of harm, kid."

Hall agreed. "And it won't cost us anything. They're throwing a wing-ding upstairs in celebration of the capture of Larry Oster. We can freeload."

Larry Oster was a dubiously comic man Adams couldn't stand, but he had just inked a long contract and the studio regarded the event as equal in importance to the signing of the Declaration of Independence. "We'll accept their whisky in lieu of medals," Adams said.

The party was large, the drinks expertly made by several professionals brought in for the purpose. Adams had a couple of excellent martinis and felt himself start to unwind. He told Mark, "No matter how we feel, the world will go on."

"Half the time I resent that point of view," Mark said.

Helen, her odious little stint completed, was on hand, lovelier in life than on the screen. Attending her was the omnipresent Mr. Blake. His attitude, Adams considered, was becoming more proprietary as the days passed. He told his wife, "Darling, you were wonderful. I've never seen a more interesting, thrill-packed program. What suspense! Would the soufflé fall or would it not? Who's writing that show now?"

"Mamie," Helen said truthfully.

"She should write mine," Adams said. "The thing I've got now will do quite a bit toward killing the industry."

"It isn't that bad," Blake said. "And you approved of it."

"That was weeks ago. At that time the dog was not a registered nurse. It could neither read nor write, nor could it tell one subway system from another. There have been changes made, brother, as you are in a position to know."

"And the latest one suggested would make a big difference."

"You couldn't be more correct. It would put me in an institution and have the network banned from the air."

"I'm afraid you might hear more about it," Blake said. "I'm under the impression B.J. spoke to Mr. G."

"It's nice to know they're friends, that this outfit is just one big and happy family."

Helen said, "Aren't you being just a little difficult, Johnny? After all, it's just another show."

"That's a good attitude," Adams said. "It'll bring back silent movies faster than anything else." He thought bitterly of the thing he was being forced to deal with now and of some of the work he and his crowd had accomplished on "Offbeat."

"You're exaggerating things, Adams," Blake said. "The show has a good rating."

"It would have a better rating if it were a better show. What someone around here fails to realize is that there are as many intelligent people with TV sets as there are less perceptive people. The earning power of the more intelligent is greater and they should logically be the primary target of advertisers."

Blake shrugged. "You can't do Shakespeare twenty-four hours every day."

"Quality is hard to come by," Adams admitted. "But

when you can't quite grasp it you can at least approach it. Banality's the easy way out." He realized he was soapboxing. He asked his wife, "Want another drink?"

She shook her head. "And maybe you'd better slow down. I think I remember hearing once or twice before that treatise on integrity by Professor Adams."

He went to the long table where drinks were being dispensed, then took his glass to a window and looked out at New York. It had attracted him years ago with its golden promises, which had never been completely fulfilled. He had served his heavy apprenticeship in summer stock and touring companies of hit plays, and had directed two Broadway productions which had not been sensational but which had been well received. He had gone into television aware of the limitations imposed by its nature but certain that there was in it room for good work. He had done some, and as a result had been given one of the network's most lucrative accounts. He'd been wary of the job at first, but there had been no valid reason for refusal. Over the months he'd discovered that he had inherited the most bothered program in the business. The sum involved was so huge that the sponsor had to be indulged, and he was perhaps the most imaginative man who had ever made eight million personal dollars dealing with such a prosaic product as soap. Adams in a relatively short time had so successfully beaten his way up the ladder that he now grasped in his sweaty little hand the colorless banner of futility.

He finished his drink and had another with Mark Hall. They talked of shows they'd like to do and never would and "Offbeat," on which Hall had worked with him. Midway through his fourth cocktail he entered happily a state of omniscience in which the obvious method of wedding commercialism with art was on the tip of his mental tongue. He was on the very verge of telling Hall the ultimate truth when a tap on his arm distracted him and he turned in annoyance.

B. J. Applegate was a short and globular man, and Adams eyed him with distaste. The congruity of his name and appearance was remarkable. If the fellow were to wear a beret with a leather tab sticking up on top, Adams thought, he would look like nothing so much as a stemmed Winesap.

Applegate smiled in the gay fashion of a mortician.

"I just wanted to say, Adams, that Mr. G. wasn't at all pleased with your tone of this morning. I thought I'd drop a friendly warning that you might hear more about it."

The truth was in Adams and he spoke it. "Your solicitude astonishes me, B.J. I really didn't know you cared."

"Flippancy is hardly the attitude to take," Applegate said. "You haven't been in this business too long, Adams. If you would be willing to take the advice of older hands you'd find the going easier. My experience in this medium ——"

Adams had some slight knowledge of the man's background. "Your experience is limited to advertising. Your creative ability is confined to the tabulation of an expense account." He turned to Hall and smiled. "Not bad, eh?"

"My opinion is this," Hall said, "and I give it freely and without hesitation: I have a wife and three ravenous children." He walked away.

Applegate's face could have served as a clinical study in blood suffusion. "You'll hear much more about this, Adams," he said, and turned away.

Adams nodded. "Undoubtedly." He finished his drink. That was one thing about an office party, he thought. Someone always got to blow his top. Today seemed to be his turn.

He suddenly remembered that he'd missed lunch and gave his attention to a table laden with small sandwiches. Helen joined him there. She was somehow without escort. "What could you possibly have said to Applegate? He looked as if the top of his head was going to blow off."

"Nothing would come out but figures," Adams said. "Statistics. Ratings. The man has a soul shaped like a dollar sign."

"Five martinis," his wife said. "I can tell by the angle of your ears. How to alienate executives. 'Boarders Away' Adams, they call him at this point."

"I just get sick of it once in a while. If they want genius at these prices they can expect a little temperament."

"But just a little, darling. And 'these prices' aren't precisely peasant's pay. At your salary you should be able to endure an occasional odd moment of frustration."

"That's not the trick. The hide of my soul is not that thin. It's simply my contention that there's no point in making a bad thing worse instead of better. What's wrong with this business is the Applegates and the Blakes. If——"

"Harry is simply trying to do a job. He has to see that the sponsor is pleased. He has a more realistic approach to this than you, Johnny."

"That the man has," Adams said. And suddenly Helen's words and the martinis combined to kindle a small flame somewhere in the back of his mind.

Helen said in a low voice, "Head for the hills, men. The hostiles are gathering."

Adams turned his head to observe the approach of a tall lean man who wore a slouch and carried a glass in his hand. Philip Gordon was well dressed and balding, and behind his horn-rimmed glasses were the wide and guileless eyes of a cardsharp.

He said, "Helen. Johnny. How are you?"

Adams said, "Still standing, sire."

"I caught a few minutes of your show today," Gordon said to Helen. "You were only great."

"I find that the kitchen is my spiritual sanctuary," Helen said demurely.

Gordon shook his head in admiration. "If only Oster could come up with a line like that." He turned to Adams. "Can't you make the change that Applegate and Blake want? From a boy to a girl, I mean?"

"In one day? I could substitute a cat for the dog, too, except that the script calls for a bark every here and there and I'm afraid it might surprise the audience." Then Adams shrugged. "I guess we could do it, though, since we'll have to fake the barks anyway. The dog is an uncooperative beast."

"The gentlemen say you're being very stubborn."

Adams said, "Look. All you need for this opus is an animal trainer well versed in child psychiatry. I've done my poor but honest best with this onion as it stands, but I've yet to perform my first miracle."

"No talent, eh?" Gordon said. "Tell you what, Johnny, I'll be around tomorrow night after the show. Stop up to my office, will you, and we'll talk it over. Forget about the switch. Take it easy, now." He walked away.

"You were charming," Helen told him. "Just charming. You missed out on a great career when you didn't join the diplomatic corps."

Adams was indignant. "What do you want me to do,

wear a small sign saying, 'Yes, sir!'? You want me to kowtow to these people just because there happens to be a little money involved?"

"Certainly," his wife said.

One drink and fifteen minutes later he encountered Blake approximately in the middle of the room. Adams said, "A small word with you."

Blake said, "What is it, Johnny?"

"Dawn just broke dimly in the east. These frequent and horrible changes your sponsor is always promoting. How many of them are actually his ideas?"

There was laughter somewhere in Blake's eyes. "I don't know what you mean, Johnny."

"It couldn't possibly be that *you* suggest some of these things to him?"

Blake shook his head, smiling now. "Certainly not. Of course, you might say that I occasionally open his avenues of thought. Make him aware of the infinite possibilities inherent in each script."

"And at the last minute."

Blake shrugged. "You know how those things are. A man can look at a thing for days and then suddenly see what should be done."

Adams nodded. "I know just how it is. You've been a great help, Blake."

The man was not smiling now. "Under the circumstances—and I'm sure you're aware of them—why should I help you?"

Adams nodded. "As you said, suddenly a man sees what should be done."

He set Blake on the seat of his pants with the finest left hook ever displayed on these premises, and he knew real pleasure. He stood there looking at the man, then became aware of the hushed room and the circle around them. Blake showed no inclination to get up. Adams spotted Mark Hall on the fringes of the crowd and walked to him.

"Let's go someplace and have a drink."

"Well, well," Hall said. "Typhoid Mary. How horrible to see you! I suppose it's a little too late to suggest I meet you at a rarely visited spot in the subway!" His manner became loyally impatient. "Come on. I happen to know a joint where they're saving a steak for a case like you."

Chapter 4

ADAMS AWOKE in the morning with a deep bank of clouds encasing his soul. He noted with no surprise that Helen was using the guest room. He fogged his way through a shower, shave, and a change of clothes, and somehow found the kitchen.

Mamie Doyle had the lemons squeezed. "If you insist on poisoning yourself I might as well help."

He made his whisky sour in concentrated silence, then tasted it. It contained hope. He turned to Mamie. "You were saying?"

"Only that I gather things from here and there. Mr. Hall putting you to bed, then the girl coming home muttering to herself about someone's broken jaw. It wasn't hers, and it doesn't seem to be yours, so there must have been a bit of trouble somewhere along the evening."

Adams threw up his hands in disgust. "She's been fighting again!" He drank deeply.

"You'll be thirty-two-years old a month from tomorrow. And that's old enough to know better."

"I'm very sick of slobbism," Adams said, half aloud. "It would be nice to know what people are doing, and all of it not behind my back. And another lemon, Mamie, if you have the strength."

"The second and the last, and then you'll eat. And maybe you'll think."

Adams had a taste of his second drink, then found his interest diverted to ham, scrambled eggs, hot biscuits and coffee. He reviewed the events of the evening before and found no room within himself for regret. He knew he was not wrong in his estimate of Applegate, that the man had all the scintillating and admirable qualities of a clod. Blake's confession that he'd been sharpshooting had certainly called for nothing less than the drastic measures which had been taken. In all justice, his words and his actions had been only the bare minimum expected of any man not dedicatedly a mouse. He attacked his food with a vigor and satisfaction that surprised both Mamie and himself and regarded with a certain amount of pride the bruised knuckles of his left hand. That there would be repercussions to his foray against the forces of stupidity and minor villainy he had no doubt, but it was a trifle late to consider consequences. He drank his coffee. The keen axe of truth had been wielded. Let the chips fall where they may.

"What chips?" Mamie asked.

He looked at her and grinned. "Excuse me, Mamie. I definitely was not referring to the biscuits." He got up. "Tell the girl bride I'll probably see her around the studio."

"From the way she spoke last night, I doubt she'll have detectives looking for you."

He stayed with the show all day, as attentive to it as a mother to a sick child. After the last rehearsal in the afternoon he released the weary but practiced cast for a few hours. He had a word of advice for the surprisingly sober dog trainer. "If that thing doesn't behave on cue he'll be a pelt in the morning." At the child-actor's mother he smiled, but he showed his teeth. Her eyes told him that she understood.

He and Mark Hall demolished a gallon of coffee between them in the interval before the show, and Adams thanked the man for having acted as a guide in the later stretches of the previous evening.

Hall said, "Your behavior, if you'll permit me to say so, *bwana,* seemed a little bit less than inspired."

"Once in a while I get fed up," was the only excuse Adams could think of.

Hall nodded. "An admirable reaction I can appreciate in others. As for myself, I'm primarily interested in getting fed."

"So I popped off. No one was hurt." He had gathered from bits of conversation overheard during the day that the only fracture Blake had suffered had been to his dignity. "What are they going to do?"

"I must admit I'm just as pleased the question concerns you and not me," Hall said. "But no matter what happens, Johnny, I'd like to go on record as saying here and now—privately, of course—that I've always liked you."

At half past seven "This Evening" went on the air. Out of the tortured maze that had been the last week miraculously emerged something that was at least coherent. Westmore Warwick hammed it, of course, but apparently the whelp possessed a bit of charm, indiscernible to Adams during the last several days, which somehow filtered through the camera. The dog was no more than ordinarily stupid, and since the remainder of the cast was adult and professional, the end result conceivably could be condoned by an audience not too sharply critical. It had one great virtue, Adams thought. It ended. And on time. He congratulated the cast, smiled in a jaundiced manner at Master Warwick, then barely retrieved several fingers in an ill-considered attempt to pat the snarling dog. "He must have known you didn't mean it," Hall said.

The weight of the fiasco lifted from his shoulders, Adams started to relax, then thought of Gordon's request to see him. He told Hall, "I'll be back with my contract or on it," and let an elevator take him up to Gordon's office.

The tall man was alone in the large, plush room. He snapped off a TV set and said, "I was watching your show. I doubt that it will win any awards for us, but it wasn't as bad as you might think. You managed to make the kid come over pretty good."

"That particular child would look much better at the bottom of a lake."

"So the epic has thrilled what we loosely term countless millions. Forget about it. Our conversation will treat of yesterday. You had a ball."

"I said a few things. It was that or choke."

Gordon leaned back in his chair and put his feet on his desk. His smile expressed admiration tinged with regret. "I hear you really clobbered Blake. I wasn't watching."

"He's been on my back for a long time."

Gordon nodded. "Sure. But the only thing is that Blake's outfit, Barlow-Madden, has these fat, juicy accounts and despite what seems to be the prevailing opinion, this business runs on money, therefore we need the Barlow-Madden pigeons. Policy dictates that our lucrative relationship with this estimable firm remain friendly and cooperative. Frankly, they find it difficult to believe we are well disposed toward them when one of our little gentlemen belts one of theirs."

"Understandable," Adams said. So Blake had made it a Federal case.

"Then there is the matter of our Mr. Applegate. Mr. Applegate resents very strongly being spoken to in the harsh terms you apparently applied. Mr. Applegate wants to resign."

"Point for our side."

Gordon shook his head. "Unfortunately not. Mr. Applegate is of incalculable value to us, in that his father-in-law is the militant possessor of a huge block of network stock and Mr. Applegate's accepted resignation would, in the unfortunate scheme of things, precede my own only by a matter of hours."

"So it's dog eat dog."

"An unfortunate simile undoubtedly prompted by your most recent encounter with the arts," Gordon said. "It's simply that I've grown to *like* having an apartment in town and a house in the country, tickets to first nights and eating at '21'. My ex-wife, I must confess, has grown selfishly endeared to mink. I know we should feel guilty about all this prosperity, but somehow we don't. Now, don't get me wrong, Johnny. I consider you a person of genuine talent and I truly regard you as a most valuable member of the staff. As a matter of fact I had you in mind for a terrific job that hasn't quite evolved yet. You're my boy, Adams, and it is with deep regret that I accept your resignation."

"You'll have to fire me," Adams said.

"Very well," Gordon agreed cheerfully. "You're fired. Now how about a drink."

An hour and four drinks later Adams took his departure, having outlined with Gordon tentative plans for a show to be called, "Life Is Intolerable." He made a beeline for Meany's and found Mark Hall comfortably on sentry duty in that understanding pub, as he had expected.

Hall took one look at him, then held out his hand. "A salute to the valiant but vanquished."

"A matter of company policy," Adams said. "Nothing personal."

"Certainly not, and I'm sure a genius-type fellow like you won't miss that personal weekly check. What now? What further barricades to storm?"

Adams tasted his drink. "I hadn't thought of that."

"If men were always to look before they leaped, the chasm between truth and ignorance would never be bridged," Hall observed. "I have no idea who said that except myself, but it's very quotable. Although it hardly solves your problem. Ever think of opening a photographic studio catering to children's portraits?"

Adams shuddered. "I've had six solid months of this," he reflected. "Twenty-six programs. Either a change or a strait jacket is indicated. What I need is a rest."

"Whether you need it or not, it seems you're going to get it. Any ideas? What does Helen have to say about all this?"

Adams realized that in his absorption with the program he had neglected to get in touch with her. He shook his head. "I'm not too sure that she's even very interested."

"Do I sense a rift?"

Adams leaned on the bar. "Things have been sliding ever since we lost the baby. Maybe I put in too much time on the job just after that. I don't know."

"I wish I could help," Hall said, "but I've found that about the best thing I can do in a case like this is keep my mouth shut."

"It always saves a lot of trouble," Adams admitted, and when Hall left he sat alone over a ruminative glass or two. The events of the last few days did not disturb him unduly, but the over-all picture was hardly satisfying. That his marriage was becoming unsuccessful was his major concern, but the fact that after years of dedication to his work he had reached the exalted stage where for an intense presentation of a scene he had to wait upon a dog's digestion was also indicative of a certain lack of progress.

When he returned to the apartment it was later than he had thought and the place was silent. The door to the guest room was closed and a sliver of light showed under it. He wondered whether or not he should tell Helen of the latest developments but decided to wait until the morning. His thoughts kept him awake far into the night.

Chapter 5

He awakened with a clear mind and some half-formed plans, and when he went into the kitchen Helen was there, looking a bit pale, he thought. She had probably heard about last evening through one of various channels. Mamie was busy at the stove, and Adams said a blanketing, "Good morning, good morning." They echoed him and Mamie brought him some fruit juice.

He said to Helen, "Mr. G. lowered the boom after the show last night."

Her voice was even. "Well, you certainly shed a few opinions. What did you expect, a raise?"

"We cleared the air," was all Adams could come up with.

"And got it," Mamie observed quietly.

Helen asked, "And what happens now? Do you have something in mind?"

"I think so," Adams said. "I've had enough of this for a while. I need a change of pace. I thought we might go up to New Hampshire for a couple of months and let things jell. I have an idea for a play I'd like to put on paper. I'd like to forget about sponsors for the time being."

He had thought of the place in New Hampshire during the night. It was a big and beat-up house high on the side of some minor mountain, and five years ago they had bought it for practically nothing. They had repaired it to the point where it was comfortably habitable, and now it was a fine spot for a couple of weeks in the summer and countless week-ends during the skiing season, when they and a sudden swarm of old friends, some of whom they actually knew pretty well, used it as a base of operations. At the moment, it seemed like a fine refuge.

Helen looked at him in surprise. After a moment she said, "Well, I guess there isn't any reason why you shouldn't go. Nothing else seems very pressing."

"I said 'we'," Adams reminded her. And this had been a part of the midnight plan. A few weeks or months alone and possibly they could regain what they'd once had. They would never find a better opportunity to try, and they could lose nothing in the attempt.

His wife looked at him. "But I have a job, remember?"

"There's no contract involved. Give them a week and they can get someone else."

"That's what I'm afraid of. And that someone else will get the lovely five hundred dollars they pay me every Friday."

Adams said, "This is important to me, Helen. That we go up there together." There was no necessity for blueprinting the thing. She knew what he meant.

She shook her head. "You talked yourself out of a good job. I've got to think of mine."

He studied her for a moment. She did not understand him. She had considered this as thoroughly as he, apparently, and had decided that New Hampshire would be of no help to them at all. He couldn't help asking, "Is it because of the job that you want to stay in town, or because of Harry Blake?"

She got up from the table. "That might be something I haven't quite figured out. At least he doesn't run off from a job just because it doesn't fully please him." She left the room.

Adams drank bitter coffee. It wasn't as much of a surprise as it might have been. The warning signals had been up for some time, now, and he had been aware of them. Love was either ready at hand or it had ceased to exist. It was a matter that would not be argued.

"That's an angry girl," Mamie said. "You'd better talk to her."

"I would if I thought it could do any good. It's a little late for talking."

The day passed quickly enough. There was a check waiting for him at the studio and he saw that Gordon had been very generous. He spent an hour at the bank going over matters in which he had heretofore exercised too little interest. He split the account evenly and he and Helen each wound up with a bit more than ten thousand dollars.

He hit four or five places around town and picked up a few tabs, and in Meany's, near the studio, he met Mark Hall. The tall man wore a glum expression.

"All I can say for you, Adams, is that you're a quitter. You're yellow and you have no guts."

"They gave you the job?"

"This week we are concerned with a beautiful young French girl who joins the *maquis* in an attempt to impersonate her brother, who is a coward. Physically, she's awkwardly prominent up front so a formless cape and a mustache are deemed necessary to hide her charms from a certain SS captain. However, this lad has been around the league for a long time, and one evening when Marie is lighting her pipe . . ." He shook his head.

Adams patted him on the shoulder. "The money is

fine, son. They make it possible for you to afford a good psychoanalyst."

"Okay. So what's with you?"

"I'm going to try the place in New Hampshire for a while. Might do me some good and I might get some work done."

"Helen going with you?"

Adams shook his head. "She's staying. She likes the show she's doing."

Hall's voice was polite. "Can't blame her. She has a nice deal there."

"Hell," Adams said, admitting the complete truth to himself for perhaps the first time, "we're through." How such a thing occurred he really wasn't sure. The sunlight faded and the small shadows grew and suddenly it was dark. Just as easy as that.

"It happens," Hall said. "It's never nice. My regrets."

Adams nodded. "Sure. Have one for the high road."

They drank and Hall tried to leave on a pleasant note. "Don't get lost in those woods. There's bound to be a story about a dog and I'll need you."

Adams went home and the atmosphere was heavy with restraint. Mamie walked about as if there were a corpse in the kitchen and Helen was polite.

Adams said, "All right. It isn't that bad. Let's see if a drink won't lift a couple of clouds."

He made three cocktails and they sipped at them. Mamie served dinner and they picked at it. Adams told briefly of how he had spent the day and acquainted Helen with the relevant financial facts.

"I'll pack tonight and leave in the morning. You sure you don't mind if I take the car?"

"I never use it," Helen said. Her eyes avoided him.

He went out and sat through a vapid movie, then went home again. The house was silent. He thought of waiting out the dark hours filled with memories and regrets and said, "The hell with this," and started to pack. It took him half an hour to assemble what he needed in a couple of bags. He could send for anything else. He left a note and a big check for Mamie in the kitchen, then lugged his bags to the street and took a cab to the garage. It was almost two o'clock when he hit the highway headed north.

He tried to pinpoint the moment where everything

had started to go seriously wrong but he could not. The fine intangible thing that held them together had been growing imperceptibly weaker, and now this minor crisis had sapped it of its last strength. You could keep it alive with countless compromises, he guessed, but it wouldn't be the same. Love would become a tolerance and all the fine strong colors would change. You'd have only a ghost of what you started with; you'd be better off unhaunted.

He'd seen it happen to other couples and had wondered at it. Now it did not seem strange or bafflingly complex. An apparently strong structure had collapsed under the punishment of incessant small blows. Except for the loss of their child, they had known no major disasters. Perhaps it had been the intense pace of his job and its insistence on his time; perhaps it had been the small conceits of a very lovely woman. He would understand it at some future date. Now he felt an almost impersonal regret and no bitterness. Subconsciously, he guessed, he had known that it might happen. It had happened. He was not suffering the shock of surprise. He drove through the long night.

Chapter 6

ADAMS ARRIVED in West Fork with the early morning and looked down on the town from a long rise. It flanked a stream which wandered through a series of high hills, and its several church spires rose against the bravely colored woods in the background. He was reminded of what Helen had said at their first glimpse of the place. "Very unoriginal. The whole thing was copied from a calendar." Well off the favored trucking routes, the town needed but two trains a day, one from the north and one from the south, to deal with its passenger traffic and the requirements of the furniture factory which was West Fork's major and only industry.

Adams wheeled down the shoulder of a great hill in search of his breakfast and found it, as he had hoped, in Mrs. Smith's restaurant on Main Street. He was greeted with quiet warmth, his wife was asked for, and he was fed an enormous and wonderful repast of sausages, pancakes and coffee. When he had finished, he called Ed Turner, who said he would be at Mrs. Smith's in ten minutes. Adams had just finished his third cup of coffee when Ed came in.

Turner was a tall man, lean and wide in the shoulders. He had made the necessary repairs when the Adams had bought their place and took general care of the house when they were away. He was a man of multiple skills and was vaguely sixty years old, give or take ten years. He said, "Hello. Up early this year," and they shook hands.

"How's the house?"

"I was up there the early part of the week. Everything's in pretty fair shape. You'll need oil soon and food now."

"Let's go up and take a look," Adams said. He paid his check and Mrs. Smith asked him, "Just up for the week end, Mr. Adams?"

"No, I think I'll stay for a while this time."

"Then you be sure to come and get a decent meal into you now and then. Unless Mrs. Adams is coming up, of course."

Adams smiled off the inquiry. He did some shopping, put some steaks and staples and several cartons of canned goods in Turner's pickup, and they drove separately up to the house. It was a mile and a half from the village, a hundred yards off a little-traveled but unusually good road. Coming upon it was always something of a surprise. It's three stories fitted snugly into a small hollow just below the crest of the hill, which shielded it from the north wind. "Mount" Holly was something of an exaggeration, but it was easily the highest prominence in the neighborhood. The view from the entrance, reaching for miles down a broad valley, had sold the place to them. That and the fact that Bald Mountain, with its fine skiing, was only eight miles to the west.

Turner was waiting for him in the driveway. The lean man said, "Always struck me this was a nice comfortable place for two people. Twenty-three rooms."

It had been empty for almost twenty years when they bought it. They used only the lower floor and the remainder of the huge pile was unheated. A half dozen rooms on the second floor were sketchily furnished and accommodated the hardier portion of the overflow on big week ends. The third floor was merely a storage bin Adams had never thoroughly explored, crowded with odds and ends accumulated over the years which he had been too lazy to throw away.

"It's an awful lot of house for what I paid for it," Adams said.

"It was too much house for anyone to buy until you came along. Bank was glad to be shed of it. Folks just don't raise them big families any more. Always seemed to me it would make a nice little hotel."

They carried the bundles in and started the oil furnace, and Adams got out a bottle and poured drinks.

Turner said, "A mite early in the day for me," and downed the whisky in a swallow. He packed a pipe, lit it, then asked, "You lose your job or have a fight with your wife?"

"Both," Adams admitted.

Turner nodded. "Happens. My wife went off with a travelin' man. Conductor on the railroad that goes through town. Must have changed his run. Ain't seen either of them for thirty years."

When Turner had left, Adams suddenly realized how tired he was. He went to bed and was asleep in a matter of minutes.

He awoke at five, bathed and shaved. Dressing in the silent house, he began to wonder exactly what he was doing here. It was true that he had an idea for a television script, but it was neither important nor exciting. He wasn't going to starve for a little while at least, and if he really wanted a job he could get one easily enough, if not with Gordon then with someone else.

Leaving New York had not been a mistake, he knew, for Helen would have been there and the pointless impulse of attempting a reconciliation would have been strengthened by their propinquity. There might have been more point in a trip to the Coast, or he might have taken a cruise. There seemed to be nothing for him here but useless memories.

He drove into town and stopped at The Tavern. Joe Cooley was a big good-looking man in his late thirties whom Adams had come to know through their years of occasional residence. He liked the low, heavy-timbered room that was somehow a reflection of Cooley's easy personality, and tonight the logs burning steadily in the big fireplace somehow dissipated the feeling of loneliness and futility he'd known earlier. He shook hands with Cooley and they exchanged felicitations regarding their wives.

"Hear Helen didn't come up with you," Cooley said.

"That's right. I have some work to do and thought I'd be better off alone."

"Well, you better get the work done before the snow flies. All those friends of yours will be crowdin' you. You won't be able to find a place to sit down. You always complain, but they always come back."

Adams thought of the mobs that annually descended on the house, of the food and liquor bills. He considered the sparsity of wholesale-type hospitality that was resident in him at the moment and the outgoing nature of his income. "They will ruin me," he muttered. "I will take to a hollow tree."

Joe Cooley polished a glass. "You mean they don't help out at all? They don't pitch into a kitty, or something?"

"It isn't that sort of a deal. Oh, they'll bring along a steak or a couple of bottles, but Helen and I make—made—a good dollar so it was just open house."

"Well, it's real nice if you can afford it. Anyway, I guess you pay enough taxes so you'll be eligible for the county almshouse in a couple of years."

"You've always been a comfort to me," Adams said.

He was enjoying the first of Cooley's excellent martinis when the woman walked in. She would have drawn attention anywhere in the world, and in Cooley's she was a bomb-burst. Tall, her face was lovely and her raven hair uncovered. There was subdued laughter in her fine eyes and full mouth and her presence seemed to charge the room with a fresh vitality. She shrugged off a short heavy coat and Adams noticed appreciatively the rich figure that graced the sweater and skirt she wore.

She said, "Mr. Cooley, hit the lady hard. Spare the vermouth." She sat at a table near Adams.

Cooley said, "Right, Miz Durant," and mixed the drink, brought it to her table. "No sense two people sittin' here and not knowin' each other. Miz Durant, Mr. Adams. He lives back in the hills somewheres. Had a fight with his wife and lost his job and came up here to hermit it."

"That's what I like about West Fork," Adams said.

"The kindly, intelligent natives who are dedicated to serving the public."

"Impertinent, too," the Durant woman said.

"Close-mouthed. Never forget that. Your private affairs are just as sacred here as they would be on the front page of any big newspaper. I mean, if you just mind your own business they mind your own business." He said to Cooley. "So Ed Turner is the new town crier. At least give me another drink."

Joe mixed the drink. "Wasn't only Ed. Mrs. Smith said you looked a little peaked this morning. Allowed as how she thought it might be wife trouble."

"I'll put a complete explanation in next week's paper. I wouldn't want anyone to feel they weren't fully informed."

"Be real neighborly of you," Cooley said. He served the drink. "Folks would take it kindly." He went back behind the bar and said casually to the beautiful woman, "Mr. Adams is a big brain. He's got a regiment falls into his place every week end there's snow and he doesn't charge them a dime. He's singin' the blues about money and he runs a flop-house for wealthy people. Can't figure him for any sense."

Adams was aware of the woman's amusement. He said, "I don't recall asking for a loan."

"You're out of a job," Joe said. "What you should do with that old fort is make a hotel out of it. These clowns come to freeload, charge them. They can afford it."

"I'll take it under consideration. I've certainly been getting enough advice about it."

"It's for free," Joe said. "Take all you can get."

Adams finished his drink and got up. "I refuse to sit around here and be insulted by the help." He turned to the beautiful woman. "Good night. If you insist on frequenting this place we'll probably meet again." He said to Cooley. "Good-bye. Please don't talk about me when I'm gone."

"Why not?" Joe asked. "We don't hit up with you city slickers but once in a while."

Adams went down the street to Mrs. Smith's and found himself to be the only customer at the moment. She greeted him with all the enthusiasm she could muster for a man who had just deserted his wife after beating her unmercifully, then told him that all she had tonight was soup, rare roast beef with mashed potatoes, creamed onions and her own pickles, apple pie and ice cream. He said he thought he could get along on that.

She had just gone to the kitchen when the Durant woman came in. She looked around the small room, saw him and smiled.

He got up and held a chair. "You might as well sit with me. No use shouting across the room."

She said, "I'd like that." When she sat down, he was newly aware of her warm beauty.

Mrs. Smith came to the table again, wearing an air of complete disapproval. When she had repeated the menu and the lovely woman had told her it sounded fine, she returned to the kitchen. The woman smiled at Adams. "You have just been discovered in *flagrante delicto*. It's a session in the stocks for you, Brother Adams, and the ducking stool for me."

"As long as you win your letter, I always say. One thing we can be sure of—there'll be no aphrodisiac in the soup." He studied the woman, the fine bone structure of the face, the intelligent eyes, the ripe, amused mouth. Perhaps it was the circumstances, but she interested him as much as anyone he had met, and his working world was a gathering place for lovely women. He said, "My name is John. They must call you something other than 'Miz Durant.' "

"Ann," she said. "But don't let Mrs. Smith hear you. Familiarity on such short acquaintance is frowned upon. But apparently you've been around here long enough to know the rules. Is it true that you're making a hotel out of some old house you bought years ago?"

"Public opinion seems to be forcing my hand. Frankly, it had never occurred to me. What are you doing in West Fork?"

She shrugged. "I passed through here once on the way to Bald Mountain for the skiing. I liked it. I was at a loose end and it seemed a good place to wait for the snow. I've been here for a couple of months. Restful. Bald Mountain tends to be a little gay and noisy."

They talked as Mrs. Smith almost reluctantly served an excellent meal. Adams found that Ann Durant had an interesting if somewhat vague background. She spoke knowingly of spots in Europe he had visited briefly, and well-known names were unobtrusive, casual adjuncts to her conversation.

When Mrs. Smith pointedly brought them separate checks, Adams picked them up.

Ann Durant shook her head. "It's not permitted after dark."

"It will make Mrs. Smith's day. Can I drive you anywhere?"

She shook her head. "Home is a short walk. I have an apartment down the street, over the bookshop. You'll have to stop by for a drink some evening. I'll ask a couple of people so that the town's foundations won't be badly shaken."

"I'd like that," Adams said.

Chapter 7

IN THE MORNING he tramped around his deserted house, examining it critically for the first time in years. During the night he had idly contemplated the suggestion that had been made to him twice the day before—that he convert the place into a small hotel. The thought amused him and he had mentally probed the possibilities. He had many friends and acquaintances who skied at Bald Mountain, so close at hand. The activities of a hotel in this country need not be confined to the snow season, either, for the entire year was beautiful.

Why not? he asked himself. He had no more than the layman's knowledge of such matters, but since it would not be an extensive operation he could see no huge difficulties. If it could be initiated at no great expense, why not? He had no income; he was, at the moment, fed up to the ears with the work he was doing. If he wanted to write, he could do it here. If he wanted to go back to New York, that was not the other end of the world. Why not?

He called Ed Turner and in an hour Adams and the lean man were going over the place thoroughly. An hour's survey disclosed that the house needed some new shingling on the west side, that the east eaves could stand some new guttering, three sills on the third floor should really be replaced, some plumbing could stand renewal, and paint would be readily acceptable in four rooms on the second floor. Floors should be sanded—"good planking in there"—stairways and hand railings might be repaired, several ceilings needed work.

"You sound as if you want to build a new San Francisco," Adams said. "Suppose I were to undertake this reclamation project. What would it cost?"

Turner rubbed his chin for a moment. "My wages, maybe fifteen hundred dollars, your time and sweat."

Adams was surprised at the modesty of the appraisal. "That's all?"

"You work cheap," Turner said. "This hotel idea of yours makes some sense." He pointed down the side of the great hill. "Plenty of room right there for some of them ski trails like they got over on Bald Mountain. Do it with a 'dozer and a couple of men, you got the time."

"In the first place, this hotel idea is everyone's but mine. In the second, I own this house and its grounds. There might be enough room here for an ice rink."

"This house and its grounds takes in half of Mount Holly. Oughta look at the deed sometime. You own all but a little patch down near Pearson's. Buy the other half of the hill and you got something."

"Buy the other half!" Adams thought of his bank account.

"Mountains come cheap. Who wants 'em?"

Adams looked at the startling size of his holdings. His eyes followed a dry creek bed all the way down, then found another line that wandered along a ridge. Both would make beautiful trails. He said. "Impossible."

"Maybe you're right to only try the hotel first, just for size. But if you make the hotel pay, that other land won't come easy." Then Turner said, "Hear you had dinner with Miz Durant last night."

"An underground as efficient as this would have had the Germans out of France in a week. And since we're all being nosey, just who is Miz Durant?"

Turner shook his head. "Sort of a mystery woman. This is just what I heard, mind you. Twenty-eight years old. Maiden name was Sanderson. Born in Columbus, Ohio, and went to high school and college there. Has two brothers and a sister an' the parents are still livin'. Went to New York about six years ago and got some sort of a job on a magazine. Worked there for two years, then met this fellow Durant. He'd made a couple of millions in plastics. Married him and they roamed around. Had a home in New

York, another in California, a big place in Europe somewhere. Divorced him maybe two years ago, traveled, then came here a couple of months back. Likes to ski, plays the piano and reads a lot. Don't really know much about her."

"So I see. The F.B.I. could do worse than employ this entire town, man, woman and child. All right, Ed. I'll think about things and call you."

Adams thought about it for the rest of the afternoon. Even as a gag it wouldn't run to much expense. He could easily picture the annoyance of the crowd that invariably descended on him with the first snow when they were told hospitality now had a price tag on it. If the thing were a flop, the improvements on the house would increase its value, in the event he wanted to sell. He didn't see how he could lose, and there was the absurd possibility that he might even make a dollar.

He went down to Cooley's early in the evening and Joe started mixing the martini as he came in the door.

The big man said, "Hi, Johnny. Hear you had dinner with Miz Durant last night."

"A very nice person," Adams said. "We decided we'd wait at least a week before we ran off to South America. There'll be an ad in the paper, of course."

"Man could do a lot worse, what with winter comin' on. How much you figure it'll cost you to break out those ski trails, once you've bought the rest of the mountain?"

"How does Turner do it? Does he beat it out on drums or on hollow logs?"

"Ed just likes to spread good news. So you're going into the hotel business for real, eh?"

"There's a rumor making the rounds to that effect. I've even heard it myself. How is it you're so enthusiastic? I'd be competition."

Joe shook his head. "I haven't any rooms, Johnny, and I'd be likely to sell a drink to your customers when they came into town." He brought the drink around the bar and set it on the table in front of Adams. "If you make money, I'll make money." He turned as a door opened.

The woman said, "Dinner's ready, Joe. Do you want it here or in the kitchen? Hello, Johnny. Good to see you."

Mary Cooley was a tall, rawboned woman in her middle thirties, as handsome as a bright autumn day. Her handclasp was strong as Adams got to his feet. Her personality had always thwarted him somehow. There was about her a sense of something withheld, just as her smile was quiet and reserved. He had thought her dull at their first few meetings and then discovered he was wrong. The fact that he didn't understand her annoyed him.

Cooley said, "I'll eat in the kitchen. Take care of our competitor. See you later, Johnny."

Mary Cooley went behind the bar and leaned on it. "And how is Helen?"

"Fine." He could see no harm in saying, "Sent her regards."

Mary nodded. "A lovely girl, Johnny. I hope there's nothing seriously wrong. I've heard the small talk, of course."

"You never know," Adams found to be the only remark that fitted the situation. "Have a good summer?"

"Fair," she said in her even voice. It was clear she was a woman unexpectant of any miracles. "The usual."

The entrance door opened then, and Ann Durant affected the room as if another log had just been thrown on the fire. The contrast between the women underscored Adams' thoughts of a moment before. They nodded to each other and Adams stood up.

"Chairman of the chair committee. What will you have?"

"A martini, please." Adams helped her with her coat and she sat down. Mary started making the drink.

Adams was enjoyably aware of the magnetism of the woman. She smiled at him. "When do the ski tows go up? I've heard all about it."

"And all about me?"

"Of course. And I suppose you're familiar with the Durant dossier?"

"There seems to be a shadow of doubt concerning your grades in grammar school, otherwise I think I'm up to date." Mary Cooley served the martini and went up to the other end of the bar and opened a magazine. Adams said, "But why West Fork? It's on the village bulletin board that you spent a lot of time in Europe. Fine skiing there."

"My ex-husband spends a great deal of time in Europe, which makes it a very small place."

"I didn't mean to intrude that far."

"It's all right. A large mistake. I finally decided that it was a little unreasonable of him to expect me to share his enthusiasm for lush Italian movie starlets. We parted on an amiable banknote." She looked at him. "I understand you've had a bit of trouble yourself."

"You can pick up the details from anyone at the post office. I don't know them myself. One of those too usual, unspectacular things. Now you see it, now you don't." It all seemed a little far away, somehow. Perhaps the distance had affected his attitude, or it might have been the fact that everything had been so gradual. He was hurt more as a man is hurt by an awaited blow rather than by an unexpected knife thrust.

Mary served their second drink and Adams said, "Why don't you stop by what seems bound to become West Fork's newest hotel? You might look around and come up with an idea or two."

"I'd like that. I always liked to advise other people about their houses."

"It's easy to find." He gave her the simple directions. "If I'm not here, I'm usually there. Eating at Mrs. Smith's tonight?"

She shook her head. "When I get sick of my own cooking I go there or to one of the places over on Bald Mountain. Tonight is a quiet home night."

Adams finished his drink, reluctant to leave her company, unable to think of any easy excuse to keep it. He got up and said, "Drop by," and then told Mary, "The drink was fine, Mary. Better than Joe's. See you later."

Her smile was as brief as usual. "Take care, Johnny."

He went down the street to Mrs. Smith's and ate in solitude. The proprietress said acidly, "Mrs. Durant isn't with you tonight?"

Adams shook his head. "I just saw her down at Joe Cooley's. She was smoking opium and I didn't think you'd want me to bring her in, the way she was behaving."

Mrs. Smith stamped daintily away, but when he paid his check the tiny woman said, "Mr. Adams, my nephew Joey is very handy with a bulldozer."

Adams was puzzled for a moment, then he said that he would keep Joey in mind. The town was far ahead of him. He went back up the hill to a long and lonely night.

Chapter 8

In the morning he called Ed Turner and met him in town. They did some extensive shopping and trucked their burdens up the hill. Work started that afternoon and Adams discovered within himself an unsuspected passion for carpentry, painting and plumbing. Turner was a craftsman and gracefully accepted his employer as an apprentice. Adams found himself carrying all the considerable burdens, on the top of the highest ladders, hack-sawing for interminable periods at the more obstinate metals they used. He loved it.

Midway through the third day, his enthusiasm sparked by his labors, he left Ed Turner at work and went into town and visited the bank. He spoke at length with the president, Ken Meadows, and the conversation was illuminating. When he left, after two hours, he had arranged for the purchase of that part of Mount Holly he did not already possess. Since he owned one half free and clear, the bank saw no reason why he would not in good time pay for the other. He would advance the purchase price, a surprisingly modest sum, against his present property. Mortgages were discussed and Adams nodded, understanding nothing.

Enjoying this strange medium and his mind geared high, he conferred with the mayor of West Fork. Jerry Olsen finally allowed as how, if the hotel were a success this season, he could persuade the board of trustees that the town should underwrite the cost of building ski trails on Mount Holly, the work to be commenced in the spring and the expense easily justified and offset by the revenue the village would potentially enjoy from skiers thereafter. "You make a go of it this year and we'll hack your hill for you next," was the way Jerry put it.

Surprised at how quickly the afternoon had passed and how favorably, he went to Cooley's in a glow. Joe was alone.

"So Ed Turner's got you workin' for him. On your money."

"Shrewd, the natives. I assume you've been briefed concerning my visit to the bank."

Joe nodded, mixing the martini. "Seems to me you paid about a thousand too much, but that's your business."

"It's mighty white of you to put it that way."

"Why the confab with Jerry Olsen?"

Adams grinned at him. "That's my secret. It might take you an hour to find out, but you'll do it on your own time." He silently toasted the slightly amazing day and said, "Give me five dollars worth of quarters and assemble another grenade. Be right back."

He went to the phone booth at the end of the room and called the New York number that had been his own. Helen answered and time paused for the briefest moment, then he told her what he had done. "It's your property as well as mine. I want your consent, of course, and you have to sign this and that."

He didn't know quite what he had expected, but her voice betrayed no emotion. She told him she considered the place his; that under the circumstances she had no interest in it; that she would have a lawyer draw up the proper papers assigning him full ownership and send them to him immediately. Adams said, all right, that he would arrange that she be paid half of what the property was now worth, the payments to be made on some installment basis. She said that was very generous of him.

He said, "Look, Helen. Why don't you come up? We could talk about a lot of things."

She hesitated for only a moment. "And go through the entire business again? No, Johnny. I think we've got a pretty good start to wherever each of us is going."

"If you change your mind, I'll be glad to hear about it."

He went out and sat at the table and tasted his drink. He felt a deep regret but the ache was dull, like that of an old wound. There was no sense of waste, either of his years or of Helen's, because the time they had spent together had been full and had enriched rather than impoverished both of them. It was just a shame it hadn't worked.

Joe Cooley said, "No soap, eh?"

Adams looked at him. "So now you have a tap on the public phone."

Cooley shook his head. "Who else would you call with

a handful of quarters? And you don't look as if you got your job back."

The mood of the afternoon had been broken and Adams drank slowly and with no pleasure. He found himself hoping that Ann Durant would drop by and thought to ask for her but did not. He talked with Joe until some other people came in, then went back to the house.

On the next day, shortly after he and Ed Turner had quit work, Adams heard a car in the driveway. It was Ann Durant. He opened the door and told her, "Welcome to the CHÂTEAU MOUNT HOLLY MOTEL BOARD AND ROOMS LADIES INVITED."

The late afternoon cold had admiringly touched her face. She looked at the house for a long moment, became aware of the valley view. "It's lovely." She grinned. "I have a better name. ADAMS' EAVES."

"Advertising people have been shot for less. Come in and look around." He was surprised to realize the pleasure he derived from her unexpected company.

They toured the house and she was amused and appreciative. He lighted the third floor and she poked around more thoroughly than he had ever done on his own. It was all odds and ends of furniture—beds and chairs and old throw rugs. She said, "Hmmm."

"That would mean what?"

"Just that you have enough stuff here to furnish the entire place. It's all good, some of it is very old, and it's as local as the trees on the hill. With just a few additions, you could decorate every empty room in the house."

He sat on an old trunk. "I might as well tell you, I'm pretty well sold on this whole idea. If I run the place free, as in the past, it'll be mobbed. If I give them decent accommodations they'll pay what they'd have to pay anywhere else. The idea of using this furniture is a great help. See what you can dream up about heating these two upper floors. Putting in an adequate plant would cost more than I'd like to spend."

"For a man in your line of work," she said, "you don't have too much imagination. Look at those." She pointed to four small pot-bellied stoves standing in a row like so many fat soldiers. "One of those in each room. Charm, my boy. And close at hand you have all the wood you'd ever need to keep a basket filled in every room. You can buy all the stoves you need around the countryside for five dollars apiece."

"That's great. Someone would have half a dozen drinks and the place would suddenly be called ADAMS' ASHES."

"Safety measures could be taken. They were in the past."

"That was before the martini became popular. Which leads me to remark that it's about that time. Come on downstairs and I'll make you one."

He made the drinks and served them in the big living room. Ann Durant pointed to the great fireplace. "You'll barbecue the steers in that, of course."

"You are now sitting in what will be the *intime* lobby. In there," he pointed to the long, reaching western room, "will be the bar. Application will be made tomorrow for the proper licenses. The bank and the mayor assure me there will be no difficulties. And speaking of steers, I'm fresh out of steaks or I'd ask you to stay to dinner. Try Mrs. Smith's with me again?"

She wrinkled her nose. "There's a certain lack of gaiety about Mrs. Smith's. I can do better than that. I have the remains of a big rib roast that's as rare as a Ming vase. It's my impression, too, that there is liquor on the premises."

"It sounds fine," Adams said. It certainly sounded much more pleasant than sitting here on a mountaintop by himself. He made another drink. "By the time you finish that I'll have erased the signs of toil."

"Don't rush. These drinks are good."

He showered and shaved and noticed with surprise that he was exercising a bit of care in the selection of a sport shirt and jacket. He went back to the living room and was aware of the amused approval in the woman's eyes.

"It's difficult to tell the classes apart, these days."

They finished the drink and Adams followed her down the hill in the new darkness. He felt better than he had in months, and it was easy to understand why. He was free of the tensions at home and at the studio; he liked the physical work he was doing; he had enormously enjoyed the absurd, for him, bit of business he had transacted the day before. For the first time in years he was relieved of the sense of immediacy. The next moment would not be the last the world knew and the fine clear air was unsponsored.

The apartment over the bookshop was surprisingly large and the furnishings represented money and taste. The motif was comfort and Adams sprawled in a big chair and said, "Nice."

"You can sit later. I'll lead you to the ice and other ingredients and you can make a batch of those fine drinks. Earn your dinner."

"Yes'm," Adams said. The kitchen was spacious and well equipped, and as he performed his pleasant chores he heard a record player start on a familiar show score.

The dinner was fine, the brandy of the best. They sat in the living room and talked, and during the hours his approval of her was solidified. Her mind was perceptive, her vision broad, her humor razor-sharp or rowdy. He was surprised when he looked at his watch and discovered that it was eleven o'clock. He finished his whisky and soda and got to his feet.

"It's been a good evening, Ann. I enjoyed it very much."

"So did I. I now consider that you owe me a home-type steak."

"A pleasant debt to repay. You can collect any evening you choose. Sooner the better."

Adams was near the door and she was close to him. It seemed a logical part of the pleasant hours that she should be in his arms. Her lips were warm and laughing, then ardent. Her body was pliant in his arms, and in a moment her hair was soft as he held her head in his hands. He said, "Hello, Annie."

Her voice was soft. "Hello, Johnny."

Chapter 9

DAWN WAS A PROMISE at the top of the sky when she murmured drowsily, "Darling, you'd better go. The town wakes early and talks late."

He kissed the tender spot between her throat and shoulder, reluctant to leave. "It isn't for nothing they call me 'Shadow' Adams. And some morning soon you must see dawn from the top of the hill."

She grinned at him. "I'll take that daring proposition under consideration, Mr. Adams."

"Pleasant dreams."

"Those I will certainly have."

The street was empty when he reached it. He saw no one as he drove out of town, and the eastern sky was flooding with light when he reached the top of the hill. He walked from the car to the house and paused to watch morning slip silently into the long valley. He examined his emotions and discovered with some surprise that remorse was not a member of their company. He had been really alone for longer than he had thought, and what he felt most deeply was a full measure of gratitude. He raised his arms above his head and stretched in profound luxury. He went into the house and in a little while fell asleep, grinning.

A few hours later Ed Turner said, "Must have had a good night's sleep. You look pleased as the lame dog that caught the rabbit."

"Let's work," Adams told him. "We must keep in mind that I have to hustle in order to make your wages."

During the month that followed, Adams labored with pleasure. The big central room of the house had become the lounge. The bar engaged the southern view and he had to admit it was a handsome enclosure, large enough to accommodate eight or ten tables. The original huge kitchen had not been altered, nor had the rest of the living quarters on the ground floor. He would have plenty of privacy. He had cornered the pot-bellied stove market and Turner had devised a simple and foolproof system that consisted of sheet metal under the stoves and piping that led to the most convenient of the house's four chimneys. All the rooms were furnished, mainly from the attic pile, in excellent taste. Ann's.

Their relationship, it seemed to Adams, was remarkable and of Ann's devising. He had not known precisely what attitude to adopt, but she had set the tone. It was easy, casual, circumspect. She made no claim on his time or attention but was a ready and gay companion, and the conventions were outwardly observed. She made suggestions about the house and was knowing with colors. Occasionally they drove over to Pine Lodge or Pepper's Inn on Bald Mountain and had dinner. Now and then they ate at his place or hers and many times he said good-bye to her when dawn hit the hilltop or while West Fork's streets were still asleep. She was a richness he fully appreciated. If his old life were finished and a new one beginning, this would be an excellent starting point.

One night she got out of bed to make them some coffee. Adams watched her put on the robe, her movements graceful and unashamed, the body lovely and proud. He said, "You have beautiful legs."

She stretched one up so that her toes rested on the bed. "I'm lucky," she smiled. "Good legs are so useful."

"Functional."

She smiled at him. "Fun." She went off and made the coffee.

When she returned he said, "What's with you, Ann?"

She shrugged, handed him his coffee and sat on the edge of the bed with her own. *"Quién sabe?* There's this and that to do, so you do it. Having money may make it more enjoyable. I'm not sure. Boredom is a relative quantity. I've known very wealthy men who got their necks broken out of ennui. Riding, racing cars, bobsledding, falling off mountains. The ribbon clerk ends his boredom with a cheap gun or with a quarter in the gas meter."

"You sound cheerful. Isn't there anything you really like to do?"

She grinned at him.

"No, seriously."

She frowned. "There might have been at one time, but I've lost it. Learn the magazine business and then give the people the true word, the facts, the real lowdown. Point up the important issues and pour on the vitriol. It seemed important. It doesn't now." She shrugged. "I've been around a little too much, I guess."

"Marriage?" he said. "Kids?"

She nodded. "Yes. But I'd have to be sure. The last one was such a fiasco." She smiled at him gently. "You a candidate?"

Adams said honestly, "I don't know."

"Take your time about making up your mind and don't be astonished if you get a big fat 'NO.' "

He grinned at her. "This is a very fair substitute."

"Don't get porky," she told him. "And don't get me wrong. I'm not a woman who likes to be alone, but I'm damned selective." She ruffled his hair and kissed him lightly on the nose. "But you're nice, Adams. Very nice."

He tried to bow and said, "Thank you, ma'am."

She set her cup on the night table and took his from him. She took off her robe before she turned off the light. She stretched and said, "Hello, Johnny."

He said, "You also have beautiful——"

Her lips smothered him.

Chapter 10

GORDON CALLED HIM late in November. "Why this exile among the reindeer?"

"You threw me out."

"You were temporarily liquidated in accordance with the ironclad rule of the over-all policy, 'Save Gordon at All Costs.' The situation that demanded you be given your freedom no longer exists. Mr. Applegate's father-in-law passed away a week ago and his stock was sold. Mr. A. is among the unemployed—a far, far better thing for him than for myself."

"I'm going to run a hotel."

"Ridiculous. It's not your medium. I can't see you passing out towels and soap. I've got a terrific program lined up and the sponsor is literate. He liked 'Offbeat.' Come home. All is forgiven."

Adams thought about it. "Maybe sometime in the future. Right now I like what I'm doing."

"Mountain fever," Gordon said. "And by the way, aren't you someplace near Bald Mountain?"

"Eight miles as the double-breasted grouch flies."

"Come snow, I'll drop in and pin you to the mat. Reserve a room for me on the first week end you have decent skiing."

"I never pictured you on skis."

"I'm only a few years older than you but I was doing the Bernese Oberland when you were on barrel staves. Don't get too immersed in that hotel nonsense!"

Adams was surprised one day when the town taxi drove up and unloaded Mamie Doyle. Her explanation was brief. "I heard some talk about a hotel. You'll need someone to cook for you. I'll want more money than I'm getting."

Adams had never envisioned such good fortune and thought joyously of the higher prices on the menus. "Great for me, but what about Helen?"

"I left enough recipes for two months and found a cook downstairs who can prepare the stuff so that it looks almost as good as my own. My public will never know the difference."

"How is Helen?" His concern was real but he was surprised at how time and absence could temper a set of values.

"She's well," Mamie said, frowning, and he detected her disappointment with the fact that the years would not stand still. "But she doesn't eat enough to keep me busy. Besides, her mother is staying with her."

"That old wombat," Adams said understandingly.

It started snowing that afternoon. Adams waved at the falling flakes and said, "Mamie, there's our fortune. Enough of that and we'll be millionaires. Well, thousandaires."

"Horrible, messy stuff."

He called Ann at five o'clock and asked if he could buy her a drink at Cooley's.

"I can do better than that," she said. "You mix as good a drink as Joe and you can do it right here. Stop in and I'll even feed the man."

When he told Mamie he wouldn't be having dinner she was tersely indignant. "You *prefer* Mrs. Smith's cooking?"

"Never. It's just that I'm having dinner with some friends." And he wondered why the plural was more convenient.

When he arrived at Ann's an hour later her manner was one of regret. "Drinks, darling, but no dinner. Durant just called. He's at Pepper's up on Bald Mountain and wants to see me about a few matters. I settled for dinner over there."

Adams said nothing. This was out of his province.

"Better than having him come here. There'd probably be a scene of some sort."

"A scene? It's been a couple of years, hasn't it?"

She nodded. "Mr. D. is the tenacious type, in spite of

his wide interests. Doesn't like the idea of losing anything he's once had, even though he has no use for it."

Adams made drinks. Ann sat down and said, "I remember a dog we once had, a young silly Labrador with instincts for laughter but none for hunting. Sidney couldn't do a thing with him but a neighbor liked the dog and thought he could train him and wanted to buy him." She tasted her drink. "Sidney wouldn't sell. He shot the dog."

"He sounds pleasant."

She frowned. "In the beginning he seemed to be. Live and learn." She looked up and smiled. "Your snow is here and the radio says it will continue. Business should boom."

"It might get off to a crawling start, anyway. I'll know more about it in the next few days."

In a little while he saw Ann off to Bald Mountain, adjuring her to drive carefully. He went back up to the house and said, "Change of plans, Mamie. Anything easy will be fine."

He mixed a drink for Mamie and himself and tried to align his thoughts regarding Ann. It was a difficult task. Durant's appearance on the scene had, in some indefinable way, complicated matters. He felt no jealousy but a sense of irritation that the pleasant round of things had been disturbed. He realized that no situation could remain static, but change had been such a large part of his life recently that he had hoped affairs could remain in this agreeable state of suspension for some little while.

Mamie served him a lovely dinner. "If the snow continues you'll be a busy woman," he said.

"A change that would suit me. I've been thinking about it. All I'll need will be a girl to wash dishes. What about the rest of this grand establishment?"

"No problem," he told her. He had made the arrangements. A couple of girls from the village would take care of dusting, cleaning, changing the linen. Two more would be on hand to serve what food would be ordered. "Those will be your departments." A local high school lad or two would attend to any heavy haulage and Joe Cooley's younger brother was willing to exercise his mastery of drinks at the bar, a handsome bit of twenty-four inch hickory planking Ed Turner had brought to light.

Mamie nodded. "It'll be fine to be busy."

The snow continued during the following day and in the afternoon Ann called him. "The encounter was no more unpleasant than usual, but just as tiring. Suppose I give you that dinner in a day or two? I think Annie caught herself a cold and a quiet at-home evening is indicated."

"Take plenty of pills," Adams advised her. "I'll stop down to see you later."

He had an excellent dinner with Mamie. She said, "It's that quiet you could hear a glass drop. Where are my customers?"

"We need a little bit more of that messy stuff. They'll be here. I hope."

He drove down to Cooley's later in the evening. The plows had been at work on the roads, meeting the trouble before it gained any headway, and he knew that in any kind of weather access to his hostelry would not be difficult.

He had a whisky and soda. Joe said, "There's your money, Johnny, falling right out of the sky. Funny thing about snow. Years ago folks had no use for it. Now it's great for business."

"It's really very fine stuff."

"Fifteen years ago Bald Mountain was a name to scare kids with. Now it's one of the fanciest places in the state. I understand Miz Durant's ex-husband is up there. Came yesterday."

"Smoke signals in the hills?"

Joe shook his head. "One of the town girls works up at Pepper's. He's going to stay on and see if this snow means business." Then he said, "Thought you might know about it."

"I'm never as well informed as you are, Joe," Adams said. "I'll undoubtedly get the hang of things after a while, but just now my intelligence system isn't what it might be." Apparently it was no secret in town that he and Ann saw each other. He could think of no reason why he should contribute to West Fork's gossip fund, but the exercise of a bit more caution was indicated. A juicy little scandal would do no one any good. It was amazing how complicated simplicity could become.

At Ann's, he found her pillow-propped on the sofa under a blanket, reading. She looked comfortable and beautiful. Adams said, "I wish all my patients looked as well as you."

"An ounce of prevention, you know. And pour yourself several ounces, by the way. It was nice of you to stop by."

He looked at her. "I hope you're kidding. You knew I'd be concerned."

"A girl never knows. But it's nice. What's new in town?"

"Apparently us," he said. "Picked up a word here and there. We are on the grapevine."

"We have been ever since that first evening in Mrs. Smith's." She looked at him. "Does it bother you?"

He shook his head. "Not a bit. I thought that you——"

"Forget about it." She grinned at him. "Kiss me and catch yourself a cold. My germs are lonesome."

On Wednesday morning it was still snowing and Adams got the first phone call. It was Strick Lewis, who ran a small and very successful advertising agency.

"Johnny! Where have you been hiding?" He hadn't seen Lewis in six months. "I called and I called and finally someone told me you'd taken to the hills. How's the weather up there?"

"Snowing like crazy," Adams said. "Has been for three days. They're packing over at Bald Mountain and they've got five inches of fresh on a six-inch base." He could almost see Lewis licking his lips.

"I did hear a rumor," Lewis lied. "Kate and I thought we might take a ride up this week end. With a few friends. Think you can put us up in that big barn, ha-ha?"

"Plenty of room. Bring one and all. The only thing is, it'll cost you. I've gone commercial."

"Old Johnny! Always a gag! Don't you worry, kid. We'll bring a couple of bottles."

There was a call later in the day from Fred Trent and another on Thursday from Henny Taylor. They were given the word, which they obviously thought hilarious. Phil Gordon called Friday and said he'd be on hand early in the morning.

Adams had Ann up to dinner on Friday. Young George Cooley was lonesome behind the bar in his white jacket and they put him to work. Ann went through the house and confirmed Adams' opinion that all was in readiness, that drapes hung correctly, that the lighting was sufficiently intimate and subdued. Then he introduced her to Mamie.

They exchanged trivialities and measured each other with the micrometers of their instincts. Adams was immoderately pleased when after three or four minutes Mamie smiled and said, "I hope you will like your dinner."

It was, of course, a minor masterpiece, created of curried chicken and exotic condiments, wild rice and a superb Roquefort salad. "Aside from being a lovely person," Ann said, "that woman is one of the world's fine cooks."

And Adams felt a bit smug later, when he had complimented Mamie on the meal. "Well," she said defiantly, "I like her."

It was nine o'clock when Strick Lewis and his wife and a few friends drifted in. Eight, altogether. There were shouts of greeting and the slapping of backs, and Lewis said, "Lord lumme, a bar and tables! The man's playing at hotel!"

"That's right," Adams told him. "Ten to fifteen bucks for a double room, take your choice. I'll accept your checks and I want to see your marriage certificates."

They stared at him. "You're kidding," Kate Lewis said.

He shook his head. "I told Strick the deal over the phone."

There was only a moment of hesitancy. Lewis looked at the bundle he held. It evidently contained several bottles. "This is a little foolish."

Adams grinned. "Drinking is permitted in the rooms."

The Henry Taylors' party was the next to arrive. Six of them. "I know we'll be a little cold, old boy," Taylor said. "But we don't mind."

"You'll warm up fast," Adams said, and gave him the bad news.

Taylor took it with good grace. "It was too good to be true. For years." He dragged from the car the half case of whisky which was his usual tribute. "This was going to be a present, but I wouldn't want to offend you." He lugged it up to his room.

Fred Trent arrived at midnight. He had only three people with him. They were a little high and decided the whole thing was a splendid idea.

"No one seems to mind," Ann said.

"Why should they? It's a nice layout and only half an hour from the best hill they could find. The same accommodations would cost them more at Bald Mountain, if they could get them. I have an idea this was a splendid thought first proposed by everyone but me. Eighteen in the trap now and there are sure to be more tomorrow who just didn't have time to phone, Johnny old kid."

Chapter 11

HE WAS RIGHT. Gordon was among the early arrivals. He eyed the place with approval, then got ready for Bald Mountain. "We'll talk later," he said. "Plenty of time, with this fine snow. They can do without me in New York for four or five days, God forbid they should find it out." He shouldered his skis. "I'm utterly exhausted and up here for a complete rest."

"This looks as if it's going to be great fun for everyone but me," Adams complained. "Everybody is out on the hill and I just sit here."

"And make money," Gordon reminded him. "The trials and tribulations of commercialism. What you deserve for giving up your amateur standing."

And late that afternoon Adams was surprised to see Gordon walk in with Ann Durant. She was lovely, looking as a beautiful woman is supposed to look in ski clothes, her color heightened by a day on the snow. "You know this peddler?" Adams asked.

Ann nodded. "We met a couple of years ago at St. Antoine when I knew very little about skiing. Phil's a real *kannonen*. He was very helpful."

Adams observed the smiles they exchanged. *What a small, small world,* he thought. He was surprised at the jealousy he felt and reminded himself that anything that had happened between them in the past, if anything had happened in the past, was strictly none of his business. He examined Gordon more closely, looking for little things that would make him selectively acceptable. He would probably pass the test.

Gordon said, "Drinks, my good man. And don't annoy the guests."

"Instantly, sahib," Adams said. He sat with them and they talked of Bald Mountain. The trails were all in wonderful shape. "Monday," Adams said, "most of this riff-raff will be out of here. Adams will hit the hill and astonish the bystanders."

"Sharp, eh?" Gordon asked.

"You will have an opportunity to watch the maestro. You will undoubtedly leave in shame the next day."

Gordon indicated the crowded room. "You hire all these people for the opening?"

"These are contented customers. Some of them have eaten. The lines to New York and Boston have been busy, extolling the food and the charm of the management. What I have on my hands is a success." Adams knew it was true. The easy atmosphere of the house and the wonderful cuisine were exerting their influence. Everyone was having a ball. Adams liked the place himself.

"And when the snow is gone?"

"The countryside is beautiful all year round and Mamie's wizardry is constant. I'm very much afraid I've fallen into a good thing."

"That's all very well, but what about me? What about the art form you deserted? What of the cameras hungry for your talents?"

Adams looked at him. "And next month another Mr. Applegate?" He shook his head. "I'm not sure, but from here it seems to me that you can take that coaxial cable and wrap it around your head. I think I like what I'm doing."

"Hear! Hear!" Ann said.

"You can't be serious," Gordon told him. "You're going to waste a talent like yours hustling baggage for drunken skiers? I'll get you a contract that will eliminate all future Mr. Applegates from your consideration."

"Maybe sometime," Adams said. "Not just now. This is interesting. I'm having fun. No one is breathing down my collar."

Gordon looked at him and shook his head. "I don't believe it. We'll go into this again. In the meantime, what is there to eat?"

"Not very much. Steaks, venison, suckling pig, lobster Newburg—stuff like that." The place was crowding up with people coming back from Bald Mountain and there were things for him to do. He said to Ann, "Let him buy your dinner. He cheated me for years. I'll be around to see you later."

In the kitchen Mamie was a busy, happy woman. "They're all not as stupid as some of them look. They like the food."

"Feed them well. They're being overcharged."

Adams visited here and there, and everyone, it seemed, was happy with the arrangements. There were adjustments to be made but they were minor and a spirit of great good will prevailed. During the later part of the evening he had to get behind the bar and help George Cooley keep abreast of the traffic. Near midnight Ann said she was tired and going home, and Gordon offered to drive down the hill behind her to guard against any mishap. "A night-cap is our only charge for such services." Ann said she would stop by the next day. Adams watched them leave and felt only a slight twinge.

Sunday was a fine and busy day. Most of the crowd had to be at work on Monday, so they came off the hill early in order to load themselves with Mamie's food and start the return trip in plenty of time. Adams booked sufficient reservations to assure him that in the next few weeks the hotel would at least maintain itself, and he knew that once these people got home and spread the word he would be in trouble. His operation would be oversubscribed and rooms would be at a premium. His thoughts wandered to next year, when his own good trails would be available. He'd have to add to the house or build something adjoining. He had a small and pleasant tiger by the tail.

By eight o'clock most of the guests had left. Adams had dinner with Ann, who had stopped by earlier for a drink. She said, "So things look fine?"

"The boniface business is booming, it seems to me. It's largely the snow, of course, but Mamie is a main factor. Also the decor, thanks to you. Also the small stoves, ditto. Sort of a plush pioneering. *Without* snow we'll do well enough."

"Then you're going to stay on?"

"I'm not fully decided," Adams said. "For years I've been running like hell to meet some type of deadline. The money's fine and the work is mostly rewarding but there have been plenty of times when I've felt like a squirrel in a revolving cage. This is a lot more solid, gives me time to think, to write if and when I want to."

"Gordon will be disappointed if you don't go back."

"He'll find someone else. I'm not that good. And speaking of Mr. G., I haven't noticed him around."

"I saw him with some people over at Bald Mountain this afternoon. Probably stayed for dinner."

It was after ten o'clock when he drove Ann down to West Fork in her car. "The walk back up the hill will do me good," he said. "I don't think I've been out of that madhouse in two days. I'm beginning to feel like a cloud of tobacco smoke filtered through a martini."

At the apartment Ann made him a tall drink and he sat in a big chair and looked at her. She was relaxed, pleasantly tired, quietly gay. He said, "Annie, you are a very toothsome wench."

She grinned and came over to him and sat on his lap. "Tell the lady more."

"You eat too much. I'll be out of house and hotel in no time if I continue to feed you on the cuff."

"A girl's got to get paid off somehow."

"I suspect you drink. There was one evening I could have sworn I smelled whisky on your breath."

"Cough syrup."

"You look too well in ski clothes. You fill out the back part too satisfactorily. Every man's eye was on you. After this you'll wear a Mother Hubbard."

"Mother Schmubbard. What's the back part for but to fill out? And tell me who was looking at me. I like to know these things."

"Also, I think you're a woman of lax morals."

"M-m-m! Now you're making sense." Her mouth was warm and fervent on his own.

It was going on four o'clock when he walked back up the long hill. West Fork was silent in the windless cold and only when he got out of town did the occasional barking of a dog break the stillness. He thought with deep affection and concern of the sleeping woman he had just left. She was puzzled, he knew, lonesome in the deep and private sense and cautious about attempting again a venture in which she had already known failure. What he shared with her was a rich companionship which could evolve into something much more powerful if they lent it their permission.

Sleep did not come easily to him. Dawn was full-blown

when he stood at the window with a cigarette and watched Gordon drive his foreign sports job into the car yard. The tall man must have run into some interesting company.

Chapter 12

MONDAY WAS CLEAR and the house was almost empty. Adams noticed that the cleaning was going well, that young George Cooley was taking an inventory of the bar. In the kitchen, Mamie was on the phone replenishing the larder. Adams listened for a moment, reminded her that it was unlikely the 1st Infantry Division would stop by for lunch, gathered himself some coffee and a snack breakfast. He called Ann to see if she wanted to go skiing with him but there was no answer. He checked the receipts for the week-end and was very pleasantly surprised. A man could make a fine living this way if he wasn't careful. Gordon appeared on the scene looking a bit the worse for wear, had two whisky sours, coffee and toast, and the two of them set out for Bald Mountain.

Adams enjoyed himself thoroughly. Gordon was an adept and they took the good trails together, running them hard after the first warm-up half hour. They quit at half past three and Adams said, "Come on. I've forgotten what it's like to buy a drink with money." They went into Pepper's Inn, near the foot of the chair lift, and had a drink at a table near the bar.

Gordon stretched his long legs. "I'm beginning to get your slant on this innkeeper deal, my boy. No insistent phones ringing, no vice presidents in charge of ulcers. I prophesy an old age for you. Which reminds me, when can I expect you back in New York?"

"Not while there's snow, anyway. Like you, I'm just starting to realize the potentials of my new enterprise." He thought with anticipation of the morrow. He'd be a bit stiff, he knew, but it would work out. "And by the way, is Ann any good? Can she really ski?"

"She's all right," Gordon said. "You slow it down just a bit and she'll stay with you." He looked at Adams. "Nice girl. A little lost."

"It might be a virtue," Adams said. "That lack of absolute assurance."

Gordon nodded. "Leaves room for development, at any rate." Then he said, "What do you hear from Helen? I don't see her often."

"Nothing." Adams was reminded again of how closely the women were linked in his mind. "I bought her share of our vast estate. It's reasonable to suppose the merger is dissolved. The courts will probably carry on from here."

"My regrets," Gordon said. "*C'est la vie.*" Then he straightened in his chair. "Speaking of the Durants, there's another."

The inclination of his head indicated a figure at the entrance. The man was tall and well built, the jaw hard, the eyes and nose hawklike, the mouth uncompromising. *Handsome,* Adams thought. *Rough.* Durant looked through the room and his eyes rested on Gordon. Durant nodded briefly, went to a distant table.

Adams said, "You know Abd El Krim?"

"I've had the dubious pleasure of meeting him. Has a warm, responsive personality. Like a glacier. Attractive, of course, and I can see how Ann could make the mistake."

Adams looked at the man across the room and felt a formless anger, a resentment compounded of shadows. He got to his feet. "Time I got back. How do I know there isn't someone anxiously waiting to pay a bill?"

They got back to the hotel near five, had a couple of cocktails, then ate some loin of pork on which Mamie had exercised more care than she would have shown in roasting her brother. Gordon talked shop and Adams listened, surprised that the subject held so little interest for him, seemed so removed.

It was seven o'clock and they were having coffee when the girl who was serving them said, "Mr. Adams, there's someone in the lounge wants to see you." Her nervousness was evident.

Adams told Gordon, "Hold the fort," and went into the lounge. There were two men there. Tom Hawley was a tall paunchy man in his late fifties. His eyes were very blue, his nose prominent. He was the chief of West Fork's three-man police force. The big man with him was dressed in the uniform of the state police.

Adams said, "Hello, Chief Hawley. Want a couple of rooms?"

Hawley shook his head. The usual laughter was absent from his eyes. "This is Sergeant Newman. Want to talk to you, Adams. Got some place a little more private?"

Adams wondered what one of his drunken guests had done. He said, "Sure. Just a minute." He went into the bar, told Gordon he'd be back, then returned and led Hawley and the state cop into his private quarters. "Drink?"

Hawley shook his head. "Not a friendly visit, Adams. Want to ask a few questions. Where were you last night?"

Adams looked at the intent faces of the men. "Why, here. Lots of people leaving, stuff like that. We were pretty busy."

"You here all night?" the state cop asked. "You didn't move from the place?"

Adams looked at the tough face, the hard eyes. He said, "Slow it down a little. What difference does it make to you? What goes on?"

Sergeant Newman said, "We'll ask the questions, Adams. You just answer them."

Adams grinned at him. "Sergeant, you've been looking at too many TV shows. Some of which I wrote. What you'll get from me is a great big nothing until I know what you're talking about."

"So we have a wise guy."

Adams shook his head. "A curious guy, maybe. What business is it of yours what I do with my time?"

The sergeant looked at him for a long moment. "Okay. Ann Durant is dead. News to you?"

Adams stared at him and the acceptance of the words was as difficult as anything he had ever attempted. They rearranged themselves in absurd patterns and made no sense at all. All he could say was, "Dead?"

The state police sergeant's voice was flat. "Yeah. Dead."

The warmth gone, the loveliness no longer existent, the gaiety stilled, the ardent mouth cold. It came through to him like that and he looked at the two men before him and had to believe it. He said, "All right. What do you want with me?"

Newman said, "The county coroner says she was murdered some time early this morning."

Adams stared at him. Not dead, as in dead. No sudden illness. No accident. Murdered.

Chief Hawley's voice came through the fog. "You were seen in town about four o'clock this morning."

About four o'clock this morning with gratitude in his heart, the memories warm and good, Ann asleep smiling. Adams said dully, "Yes."

"You weren't walking a dog," Newman said.

"That's right."

"Mrs. Greer saw you," Hawley said. "She lives on Main and Cedar, only a block from where Miz Durant lives. Lived. And then Alice Stanton saw you. Her place is out near the edge of town."

The good grin, the lovely personal scent—those were gone and he would never know them again. Whatever Ann had been looking for she would never find.

Adams came back to the moment. "What happened?"

Newman answered him. "Suppose you tell us."

Adams stared at him, finally getting the implication. "Don't be ridiculous." He began to realize some of the difficulties the immediate future would present. "What do you want with me?"

Newman's voice was even and hard. "We'd like you to tell us about the murder."

"You're being stupid," Adams said, and derived some satisfaction as he watched the big man flush with anger. "What do you want up here?"

Hawley looked at Newman, then said, "I guess you're under arrest, Mr. Adams. We locate you at the scene just about the time the coroner says the murder happened."

The whole thing was becoming more of a nightmare. Adams could only say, "You locate *me* there! How many people are there in West Fork? About fifteen hundred? They were all pretty close."

Hawley nodded. "Sure, Mr. Adams. But there weren't none of them stayin' with Miz Durant all night, five, six times durin' the last month. Not countin' the times she stayed up here."

It started to bite in, then. The privacy that would no longer be private—the intimacy that would become a public topic—a darkness blazoned into headlines—the soft and whispered hours shouted into the streets. *And Ann gone. And Ann gone.*

His anger was not at these men but at the destruction that had been committed, and the anger was a cold and intense thing such as he had never known. He could not believe that Ann had ever done anything to merit such a termination. He had known her well and well, had listened to her dreamings, her small apologies for the past. There had been nothing in her that would serve violence.

He said, "All right. What happens now?"

"We don't have any proper place to hold you," Hawley said. "Looks like we'll have to take you over to Winslow." It was the county seat, fifteen miles away.

Adams was slowly coming out of his shock. "Give me a couple of minutes to clear things up around here."

Hawley nodded. "Take your time." The state cop said nothing.

Adams went to the kitchen and explained the whole thing to Mamie. She was horrified. "That lovely girl! And to think that just the other night . . ."

"You'll have to take care of things until I get back. I don't know how long that will be. Think you can handle it?"

Mamie nodded, her tears flowing freely. "I'll manage."

In the bar, Adams told Gordon what had happened. The man was as unbelieving as he had been. "It's incredible! Some sort of awful mistake. It simply couldn't happen, Johnny."

"These men aren't joking. Mamie will take care of you. I don't know how long I'll be gone."

Gordon was on his feet. "You don't say anything, Johnny. Understand? I'll get on the phone right now and in the morning this place will be swarming with lawyers."

Adams thought about that. "No, I guess not. If this is going to be my town I think I'll do it their way. Never mind the phone call. Maybe later, if things get really rough. I really don't know what these people want, yet."

"You're crazy! We've got a big fat legal department that sits around on its collective duff doing nothing but drawing up contracts no one can understand. I've always wanted to see if any of those jokers was good for something else."

Adams shook his head. "You just sit still. We'll see what happens."

Gordon swore harshly. "Ann Durant. That girl. What the hell happened?"

"I don't know. They won't tell me. They just ask."

"What are they going to do with you?"

"I don't know the procedure. It seems they don't have

any escape-proof jail in West Fork, so they're taking me over to Winslow. I guess that in the morning I can get hold of a lawyer and find out more about it."

"A lawyer. Some backwoods blabbermouth who got his degree from a mail-order school and doesn't know a writ from a rat! Anyway, I'll be here. Keep in touch and tell me what I can do."

Adams said, "All right," and went out to Hawley and the state cop. "I guess that's about it. Let's go wherever we're going."

Chapter 13

SERGEANT NEWMAN DROVE and Adams sat beside him, with Hawley in the rear seat. During the half-hour ride neither of the officers spoke and Adams made an attempt to understand what had happened. That Ann was dead was incredible, but it must be true. That he should be accused of her murder was equally inconceivable but a very evident fact. His sense of loss was his predominant emotion and his anger walked beside it. His acceptance of the entire situation was complete now, after this little time, and the *why's* and the *who's* were beginning to gather. He didn't even know the answer to the very important *how*.

He asked the man beside him, "How did Mrs. Durant die?"

"We'll get around to that later," Newman said. "You're not handing out any information. Don't expect any from us."

His answer gave Adams a brief insight into what lay before him. He wasn't dealing with his equals any longer but with police officers who seemed to believe he had committed a murder. It made one hell of a lot of difference, he realized.

At Winslow, the police department occupied the basement of the courthouse building, and Adams was led down there. A reception committee was on hand to greet them, three men in civilian clothes and another state trooper in uniform, a lieutenant. He was herded through a succession of offices to a small room which held only a large table and several chairs.

One of the men identified himself. "My name is Sands. I'm the county district attorney." He was of medium height, balding, with a thin face and a nervous mouth, and seemed to be in his middle forties. He said, "All right, Adams. Why did you strangle the Durant woman?"

Strangled. Hate-filled hands on that lovely throat. Obliteration while staring at the destroyer. The light turning red, then black, and no breath for the screaming lungs.

Adams shuddered, then shook his head. "I didn't strangle her."

"Come on," Sands said. "Get it over with fast and we can all get some sleep. I don't even care right now why you did it. But you killed her, didn't you?"

Adams shook his head. The whole thing was going too fast for him. First the stated fact of Ann's death, so difficult to accept, and then the insane accusation. There should be time for the one, he thought, before you encountered the other. A man should not be expected to deal with two such monstrous things at once. He said, "No. I don't know anything about it."

Sands's manner was the patient attitude of a parent explaining to a lying small boy that the method of his transgression was clearly evident. "You were with her, you both were drinking, you had a quarrel and you grabbed her by the throat. Before you knew what was going on it was all over. Right?"

And Adams thought of Gordon's parting admonition, *"Don't say anything."* In the face of this concentrated disbelief it seemed the safest thing to do. He said, "I'd like to get in touch with a lawyer."

Sands smiled. "Ah, a lawyer. If you didn't do it, Adams, what do you want with a lawyer?"

"I'd like a little friendly company around here."

Sands snorted. "You want a lawyer so soon? You can talk, can't you? You can tell us what happened, how you did it, what the circumstances were?"

"I think a lawyer would be a fine idea."

"The lawyer is for later, to try to do as much for you as he can. Not for now. Now is for you to tell us all about it, while it's still fresh in your mind. A lawyer won't be able to help you until you talk to us."

"I've talked to you. I've told you I had nothing to do with it. Where does that get me? You've got your mind made up that I did this thing and it's clear that nothing I can say will change your opinion."

Sands had been sitting on the edge of the table. He got up and paced across the room and came back. "Adams, this isn't the first time a man has killed a woman. It happens. Maybe there were extenuating circumstances. She might have threatened you with a knife or something, for all I know. Maybe you were protecting yourself."

Adams looked at him and said nothing.

Sands let his expression show that his patience was being taxed. "Look, Adams. You were seen leaving Durant's apartment at the approximate time the coroner says she was killed. You'd been there before. Don't try to give us a snow job. You killed her. We know it, you know it. All you have to do is admit it. Just confess and keep it all simple."

Adams shook his head in amazement. "Admit to something I didn't do and keep it all simple? You must be out of your mind, Sands."

The man straightened as if he'd been cut across the back with a lash. "All right, you smart bastard. If you want it the tough way you can have it like that. We've got all the time in the world."

"Okay. Just so we don't keep it simple." Then he thought of something. "There were people who saw me an hour ago who'll swear there wasn't a mark on me."

"Smart!" Sands said. "A real smart bastard." His smile was not a pleasant thing. "We wouldn't touch anything like you, Adams. You just answer a few questions."

"Maybe. When I see a lawyer."

Sands sat on the edge of the table and lit a cigarette. "This Durant, Adams. What was she like?"

Adams said nothing.

"She'd been around. I imagine it must have been an interesting sackful."

Adams stared at him and could feel the anger mounting. Not cold, now, but hot and immediate and demand ing. He killed it, cooled it, recognizing the trap. He hoisted up a chair inside himself and sat there observing and unmoved. But remembering. Remembering every word.

Adams didn't know how long it went on. They used relays, a couple of men who apparently were from Sand's office. Chief Hawley left very early during the proceedings. Adams noticed that the state police lieutenant, whom he had heard addressed as Mayo, stayed in the background and said nothing. The questions came at him insistently, repeatedly. How long had he known Ann? How well had he known her? Had he ever met her before coming to West Fork? Why had he strangled her?

The inquisitors began to probe deeper, and Adams sat there controlling the anger. Had he found the woman with another man? Other men? A little pregnancy imminent? Maybe she wanted some money from him?

Sands became an understanding man of the world. "Hell, Adams, we all know how these things happen. You think you've got a hunk of stuff all for your own and suddenly discover it's on the open market. Of course a man gets sore. He starts to shout and the broad gets scared and picks up a knife. She comes at him and he grabs her and bingo! The thing is over before he's had a chance to think. That'd be your out, boy."

Adams said nothing, wondering how long it would go on, wondering how much abuse a man could take, how far discoloration and distortion could go. There had been nothing sacred about his relationship with Ann, but now it had become a slack-jawed gaping thing under the bright light in the hungry voices of these men.

A man took Sands aside and whispered to him, and in a moment the district attorney was back. "The coroner says Durant might have been raped, Adams. You don't mean to tell me that after all this time you had to rape her!"

The two men who evidently worked for Sands laughed loudly with him. Adams stared at them, knowing real hatred. He could taste it. He stared at them. But he remained silent. The state police lieutenant lit a cigarette, averting his eyes.

They let him go, finally. He could see the vast weariness that was part of him now mirrored in their faces. He was led to a small cell that boasted a cot and he lay down, the ugliness of the whole thing pressing in on him, his bitterness a hard pillow. He knew he could not sleep.

But he did, and awakened cold and not remembering for a moment until it hit into him again. He was stiff and his soul was tired, and he said to the officer who had shaken him and who now stared at him curiously, "I want to use a phone."

The man said, "Sure. You've got plenty of time. The toilet's down the hall. You want to use it?"

Adams washed and ran his fingers through his hair. The paper towel left small tufts on his stubble of beard. His eyes were bloodshot and he looked as if he had been on a drunk. His watch told him that it was almost eight o'clock.

The uniformed man walked him back to the cell. "Mr. Sands wants to see you at nine o'clock. I can get you coffee if you want."

Adams nodded. He gave the man a bill. "Plenty of coffee, black. Couple of doughnuts. Cigarettes."

He sat on the cot and tried to figure what was happening to him. He had only a casual knowledge of police procedure and was uncertain of what would occur next. He felt quite sure, somehow, that in following Gordon's advice to keep his mouth shut he had not made a mistake. His presence at Ann's would certainly be difficult to explain, and he knew that Sands fully believed him guilty of the murder. It was an obvious thing to the district attorney, and the quicker he could get a confession from Adams the more easily the case could progress.

His coffee, doughnuts and cigarettes came and he thanked the man and offered him a dollar from the change, which was refused. The coffee was hot and fresh and it brought life back into him. He wondered what Sands would have to say that he hadn't said last night. He remembered some of the questions and cursed Sands silently and then began again to be objective about it. The man had been trying to arouse his anger so that he would say the one irretrievable sentence, had been digging his probe deeper and deeper into the fresh wound. Maybe that was the way the job had to be done. But Adams' anger at the man persisted. He could not excuse him.

In a surprisingly short time the cop who had brought him the coffee was at the cell door again, unlocking it. He said, "Mr. Sands wants to see you now."

They went to an office on the second floor and Sands was there. He looked tired, but he'd at least had a chance to shave and change his clothes. He said, "Adams, I'll get to you and I'll get to you good, but I can't hold you unless you're arraigned and I don't want any smart lawyer walking in here with a writ. The judge'll be here at ten o'clock and I've got to wait for that." He moved his hand. "There's a phone."

Adams called the West Fork bank and asked for Ken Meadows. The president came on the wire quickly. Adams identified himself and said, "You people must know a lawyer. I'm in trouble over at Winslow."

"I've heard something about it," Meadows said. "Bill Tate does most of our work for us. Little young, but we like him. You want him?"

"I want him fast."

"We'll send him right over, son."

Adams cradled the phone and looked at Sands. The man said, "Adams, why be so stupid? This is all going to come out in the wash."

"I hope so. I'm getting a little tired of it."

"Why don't you make it easy on yourself and tell us why you killed that rich tramp?"

Adams called him a short, ugly name.

Sands stared at him and said, "Get out of here."

Back in the cell, the anger subsiding, Adams wondered how long Tate would be, what he would be like, what he would be able to do. He thought of Ann again and in spite of himself reviewed their time together, the warmth of it and the lack of any sort of conflict. He thought of that lovely body now, under the coroner's cold care, and shuddered.

It was little more than half an hour after the call when Tate was admitted to the cell. He was tall, slim and dark, in his early thirties. He held out his hand and Adams took it.

"I'm Bill Tate. Hear you're in a jam." There was a quality about the man Adams liked instantly. "All I know is gossip," Tate said. "We haven't got much time. I've got to know exactly what you told these people."

Adams said, "Nothing."

Tate stared at him and a slow smile broke on his face. "Nothing at all?"

"Several people evidently saw me in West Fork around four o'clock yesterday morning. I was there about that time. That I admitted. I said nothing else. Except a personal remark or two to Sands."

Tate grinned. "That I can understand. Let's go up and see that man and see what sort of a thing he has."

The turnkey let them out and walked with them to Sands's office. The district attorney was there with the state police lieutenant, Mayo.

Tate said, "Well, here we are. What's the story? What are you going to charge him with, Sands?"

Sands managed to look both smug and angry. "Murder, is all."

Tate said simply, "Why?"

"Plenty of reasons. In the first place, lover boy here was practically living with the woman. His fingerprints are all over the apartment. We got his from stuff he handled here last evening. He was seen in West Fork at four o'clock in the morning by a couple of people—a Mrs. Greer and a Miss Stanton. Four o'clock is approximately the time the woman was killed. The whole thing is obvious. He quarreled with her and strangled her. Don't get yourself into a sweat about it, Tate. If you had any sense you'd leave this thing alone."

Tate said, "Who told you Adams was Ann Durant's lover?"

Sands shrugged. "Common knowledge."

"Do you know where old Mrs. Greer lives?" Tate asked. "A block and a half from the Durant apartment and around a corner. Do you have any idea where Alice Stanton lives? A mile away. Who saw him leave the apartment? Who heard this big quarrel you're talking about? What you know positively is that at some time or other Adams evidently visited the apartment, since his fingerprints are in it. You say."

Sands was standing, now. "Look here, Tate. I——"

Tate interrupted him. "You know what I think you ought to charge Adams with? Mopery. Being on the street at four o'clock in the morning. You might make that stick. Although I can't think of any West Fork law against it."

Sands stared at him, his face paling. "What are you trying to feed me, Tate? You live in West Fork. You know all about this man and the Durant woman."

Tate smiled at him and there was a touch of condescension in his expression. "I know all about them? Do you think I pay a great deal of attention to old women's gossip? I never saw Adams go into Mrs. Durant's apartment. I never saw Adams leave Mrs. Durant's apartment." He leaned on Sands's desk. "I never saw them make love."

Sands stared at him for a moment, then turned to the state police lieutenant. But Mayo shook his head. "We've got men working on it, but right now you know just as much as I do."

Sands regarded him with indignation for a moment, and then turned as a man entered the room. The man said, "Judge Kenyon's in the small courtroom. Says he hopes you won't take all day."

Adams watched the hesitancy walk into Sands's eyes and stay there for a moment. Then the man got to his feet. "Let's go."

Judge Kenyon was a man in his late fifties. He looked over his spectacles at the district attorney. "Well, Mr. Sands, I understand you have a little business for me."

Sands told his story, and as he spoke, Adams realized that the man had very few cogent facts at his disposal. There was this rumor and that rumor, but the only item that made any sense was that Adams had been seen in West Fork about the time Ann Durant had died.

At one point in Sands's discourse Tate interrupted to say, "Gossip, your honor. Hearsay."

The judge looked at him, then returned his attention to Sands. The district attorney finished with, "I'd like this man charged with manslaughter." Adams was surprised at the reduction in charge.

Tate spoke for a few minutes. His conclusion was, "Your honor, I think this charge should be dismissed."

The judge nodded. "Think so myself."

Sands was flushed, but he said, "Then I'd like him held as a material witness."

The judge nodded again. "Makes a little more sense." He looked at Adams. "Inquired about you when I knew what was coming up. Seem to be a soundly established young man. Don't intend to do any traveling, do you?"

"No, your honor."

Judge Kenyon fingered his lip for a moment. "Looks like all your assets are in West Fork and you seem to value them highly. Let's put bail at about fifty thousand dollars. That might keep you in town."

Sands made a gesture. "Your honor, I'd like this man held in no bail."

Judge Kenyon peered over the bench. "Mr. Sands, on the evidence that you have presented, this man in all probability should not be held at all. However, I recognize the importance of his relation to the deceased. Fifty thousand dollars seems a sufficient anchor to the movements of a young man with his evident intentions for the future."

Sands stepped back, anger in his eyes. He glanced at Adams, and Adams could feel his frustration like a blow.

Tate reached into his pocket and withdrew an envelope. From it he took a check and placed it before the judge. "Certified. On the West Fork Bank, of which I am a representative." Then he shook his head and muttered to Adams, "Ken Meadows must be a mind reader. Said this was about half of what your property would be worth."

"No one ever assessed me at anything approaching those figures. I'm very surprised."

The judge got up, handed the check to a clerk. "Guess that will be all, gentlemen." He left the small room.

Sands looked at Adams. "I'll be seeing a lot more of you, mister."

Chapter 14

ADAMS SAT IN COOLEY'S and it occurred to him how different things were now. A thought hit him with the force of a punch in the mouth. Did Joe think he had killed Ann Durant? Everything would be different now. You'd go around measuring people, noting the presence or absence of accusation in their eyes. There seemed to be none in Joe's. He couldn't be quite sure. He was new at this business and would have to learn it.

Joe said, "What will it be?"

"Bourbon. A big one. The night was long, Joseph."

Joe brought a huge drink to the table. "Get it down. You're drinkin' on me today."

Adams drank. The liquor warmed him quickly, took away some of the inner numbness. He said, "I suppose you've heard the whole story."

Joe nodded. "I guess you know this town by now."

Adams thought about that. He said, "I guess I do." Women peering out of windows in the dead of night, hoping for something to break the aged monotony of their lives. The sick and the sterile of mind, finding evil in the happiness of the more fortunate.

"They give you a hard time over at Winslow?"

Adams thought about that for a long moment. Sands and his two men probing through the hours. It had to be done, he supposed, but there certainly should be some other method. He shook his head. "They just did what they had to." He finished his drink and said, "I'll have another one of those, Joe." He got up and went to the phone and called the big house on the hill. Mamie answered and he explained that he was all right, that he wanted someone to come down and get him. "Is Gordon around or did he go to Bald Mountain?"

"He hasn't gone out."

"Ask him to ride down. He might as well be of some use. And Mamie, I could use a good lunch in about an hour."

He went back to the table, thinking absently of the fine time he and Gordon had had over on Bald Mountain yesterday. *Only yesterday?* How the world could change in a day. Yesterday had been hours of snow and clean sky and the expectation of seeing Ann in the evening. Yesterday you had said hello to people and smiled at them and today you watched their eyes and wondered which of them were your friends. And then you wondered where they had been and what they had been doing during some fearsome hour. And you remembered Ann.

Joe Cooley said, "What happens now?"

Adams shook his head. "I don't know. Bill Tate isn't sure. By the way, he's a nice guy."

Joe nodded. "West Fork kid. Went away to school, working for some law firm in Boston for a few years, then came back here. Bank gives him quite a bit of work, I guess, and he's picked up a lot of business on the side." He polished a glass. "Figured you'd have some of those big New York lawyers up here by now."

Adams said, "He'll do for me. I'm a local boy myself."

Cooley was silent for a moment, then he said, "Look, Johnny. I guess you're fixed all right, but I've got a couple of thousand that isn't making any muscles. If you need——"

"Thank you, Joe, but it's all right. I appreciate it!" It was another warm spot in the day.

"Thought I'd let you know."

Mary Cooley came into the room, then. She walked

over and put her hand on Adams' arm. She said very quietly, "Poor Johnny. I'm very sorry, Johnny."

Adams looked at her and he could not be mistaken about what he saw in those eyes. This was a member of the band that would stick. There would be no question here because there was no doubt. There had been no difficult process of thought, no tortured conclusion reached, simply because it had not been necessary. Mary knew. He touched the back of her hand. "Thank you, Mary."

There was something besides compassion in her eyes. She started to speak, then shook her head slightly and turned away, her shoulders slightly bowed.

Gordon came in then, tall and lanky. He took a chair next to Adams. "What's the score, boy? Were they rough on you?"

Adams told the story briefly. "It was a little rough. Nothing to scream about."

"This lawyer. Is he any good?"

Adams reviewed his brief acquaintance with Bill Tate. "I think so. I have an idea he's very good."

Gordon shook his head. "I still can't believe it. I'm getting a little used to the idea but it's tough to take. That lovely girl."

And then the thought hit Adams suddenly. Gordon had come in long after Adams had arrived at the hill, the night Ann had been killed. He remembered smoking a cigarette and watching Gordon park his car. And Gordon had known Ann before. Years before. What if there had been something serious between them, and Gordon, still hoping, had discovered her relationship with Adams and in some drunken fury had strangled her? Gordon didn't look like a man who would murder a beautiful woman. But then, who did?

Adams said, "How well did you know her, Phil?"

"Just about well enough to know how nice she was. Couple of years ago I took a month off and went to Europe. It was a little business but most of it was skiing. The Arlberg, the Oberland. She and her husband were doing the same thing and I'd see them here and there. We were all in St. Antoine for three or four days and I had drinks with them a few times. That well."

A couple of years ago. Just about the time when Ann and her husband must have been contemplating divorce.

And Gordon was an attractive man, the sort of person who could easily appeal to a woman disillusioned, disappointed, a little frantic with the collapse of a marriage.

Adams wondered, and if he were to express his doubts, he would have no way of knowing whether or not Gordon's reply was the truth. It was something to think about, something Bill Tate should know. It was strange how a single day could change your values. Now you could not trust a man you liked; faith was a word you looked upon with discredit; truth was suspect.

He introduced Gordon to the Cooleys and the tall man had a drink while Adams was finishing his second.

Gordon said, "What gets me is why they pushed this thing on you."

Well, maybe Gordon didn't know. Whether he knew or not, he had said the absolutely correct thing. Which was normal with Gordon. Adams said, "I left Ann's place very late. About the time the murder was committed. Someone saw me on the street."

Gordon looked at him and said, "Oh?" There was all the sophistication of Gordon's life in the word. "I didn't know, Johnny."

He didn't know. Or did he? It was a most interesting question. Adams said, "Finish that. I understand there's some up on the hill. I'm hungry as hell."

They said good-bye to the Cooleys. Mary's eyes were filled with pity and with worry.

When they arrived at the house it seemed to Adams that they'd been away for weeks. The house had not changed, but the world outside it had. Mamie met him at the door, her eyes inflamed, and Adams held her in his arms and patted her back.

"All right, Mamie. Everything is going to work out. You go and get my lunch and I'll get you a drink."

"Johnny, I still don't believe it. That lovely girl."

He said very quietly, "Mamie, I didn't do it."

She pushed herself away from him with a sudden violence. She stared at him as if he had struck her. "Johnny Adams, I never thought you'd say a thing like that to me." She turned and walked away and Adams could feel his face burning.

He had lunch with Gordon and it was not a happy affair. He knew enough not to go to the kitchen but was sure that given an hour or two, Mamie would forgive him. Gordon argued again about bringing some expensive and idle legal talent up from New York but Adams vetoed the idea.

"What good would they do? The whole thing sounds like a TV show, 'I Was There.' None of your legal beagles could discount that fact. It's all very simple. I have no way to account for my time, no alibi. I can't even be indignant that some people think I did it."

"We could juice things up. With six people looking for something, their chances of finding it are better than one person's."

"We'll wait. Don't think I'm being either stubborn or heroic. If things get really rough I'll scream for help. At the moment I believe things are going as well as could be expected."

"What are you going to do now, sleep?"

Adams thought about it. He was tired, but not to the point where sleep would reach him through his thoughts. "Wait until I get some clothes on and I'll run your ears off over on Bald Mountain."

And when they were on the mountain, hitting the two tough trails, Adams knew he hadn't made a mistake in coming here. The cold air, the beautiful snow conditions, the necessity to concentrate completely, all these things freed his mind for a few hours from the sudden intolerable burdens. When dusk intruded and they had to stop, he felt refreshed and renewed. Back at the hotel, a shower and a change of clothes further convinced him that the world might still be sane.

He had a drink with Gordon in the bar, then took a chance and brought one in to Mamie in the kitchen. She accepted it and said, "I'm sorry about before, Johnny, but you should have known better than to say anything like that."

"Of course I should have known. Forgive me, Mamie." Her eyes told him he had been shriven.

Back in the bar, he told Gordon, "I hope you don't mind, but this lawyer, Bill Tate, is coming over for dinner. We have a lot of things to talk over."

"As long as he knows what he's doing. This is no spot for some rustic, faltering Daniel muttering platitudes. I don't want to see you hung, or whatever final rite they employ in this wilderness, if only because I want you back on the job. As a cadaver you are worthless to the world of communications. Also, I like to think that such a fine skier belongs on top of the snow rather than under it."

"Your concern is touching."

Gordon said, "Hell, Johnny. I'm just worried."

And Adams knew it again; the miserable doubt, the nagging possibility that the man was playing a part. There could never be a return to things as they had been.

Bill Tate was on time and had a drink at their table. Adams made the introductions and Gordon excused himself. "You have a nice place here."

"I hope I can stay around long enough to enjoy it."

"This morning I mentioned detectives. Reasonably, the attention of the police is concentrated on you. With what they know about you now and with what they will learn, it's logical for them to assume that you're their boy."

"Makes me feel like a target on a rifle range."

"We know you didn't do it. But someone did. Our best defense is an offense. Find out who the murderer is. The police can't be expected to be as objective about this as they would be if they had *no* suspect. You stand out like a horse in a telephone booth and they can't keep their eyes off you because they're only human."

Adams nodded. It was something he'd had no trouble figuring out for himself.

"So, soon after I left you I decided we needed help. I called a firm of detectives who'd done some work for me in Boston. They're very capable, very discreet. And very expensive."

Adams shrugged. "You can't take it with you."

"There's a man up at Bald Mountain already. The technique is very professional and you and I would not be able to accomplish nearly so much as he, even if we were not known there. Within a day or so we will be completely informed as to Mr. Durant's movements on the night of December fifteenth, his general personality and temper, and through an agency branch in New York his income, his past, and where his most interesting wens are located. Another gentleman is presently hard at work in our own humble village, learning what there is to be learned. Have you thought of anything else?"

Adams felt a bit like Judas. "It's an impossible thing to consider, but the man you just met, Phil Gordon, is a friend. He met Ann Durant in Europe several years ago, then again right here the other night."

"Details on Mr. Gordon, please."

Adams told him as much as he knew, including Gordon's late arrival on the fatal night, and Tate, said, "The New York people can take care of the background and on-the-spot sleuths will attend to his local movements. Any more little gems?"

"Something you ought to know regarding my hypothetical motive. My wife and I have been separated for months. Division of property, things like that. Divorce is just around the corner."

Tate said, "What does one know! Would she testify to that?"

"Certainly. So would the cook who was with us for years and is at the moment preparing something succulent right out in the kitchen."

Tate leaned back in his chair. "This was a situation that had developed before you met Mrs. Durant?"

Adams thought about it and said, "Yes. It had been brewing for some time. Actually since we lost a child several years ago."

Tate looked at him. "You know I don't mean to sound cynical, but that's the best news I've had today. It's something Sands doesn't know about. He'll go to a lot of work building something I can destroy in five minutes."

"Here comes some food. Destroy that."

They fed on onion soup, native wild duck stuffed with wild rice, and various extremely interesting oddments. Tate came up for a breath and shook his head in appreciative wonder.

"It might ease the pressure if we got Sands to have dinner here."

They were on coffee and brandy when Tate said, "Probably the whole structure of this business rests upon a fact which I have to know before the police or Sands extract it from you by one means or another. Were you and Mrs. Durant 'intimate'?"

Adams said simply, "Yes."

Tate said, "How impersonal can you get? It's why I hate to do work for friends. All right. That's something you don't have to tell them under ordinary questioning. Your silence, of course, will give them all they want to know, but it might be less painful for you that way. You sign absolutely nothing I haven't read. That you were in the apartment that night you will eventually be forced to admit, because they'll pin you there by fingerprints on unwashed glasses, on cigarette stubs, on the daily newspapers, on used tissues. Don't deny your presence but delay the admission until you see what they have. There will be ambiguous questions you'll have to treat with care and anything you don't understand don't answer. I can't be with you all the time, of course, and just to sit there like a dummy isn't always the wisest thing in the world. Don't try to be clever with them because this is their business, not yours. Be careful, and when things look real rough imitate a clam."

Adams was finally feeling the effects of the day. He tried to concentrate on what Tate was telling him, but it was an effort. His mind had been besieged by strange facts for too many hours and he was physically tired from his work on Bald Mountain.

Tate said, "The newspapers been bothering you?"

"That's all I need. No, not yet."

"They will. . . . Just tell them nothing. It won't discourage them for a while but they'll finally get the idea." He rose to his feet. "Johnny, thanks for a wonderful dinner. It's silly to tell you not to worry, but we'll beat this thing."

Adams nodded and managed a grin. "I hope so."

Tate gave him a business card. "Couple of phone numbers on it. You can usually reach me at one of them. Take it easy. I'll be in touch."

Adams saw him to the door and went back into the bar. Gordon had finished dinner and Adams sat with him. Gordon said, "He looks a little young to me."

"Well, this is the first time I've ever been accused of murder. You've got to start somewhere."

"Very funny. You sure he doesn't need help?"

"He's all right. You just leave me and the counsel for the defense alone. I've had enough trouble in the past with sponsors."

He was suddenly aware of someone standing beside him. A man said, "Are you Adams?"

He looked up and recognized Ann Durant's former husband. He had not seen the man come in. He said, "Yes, I'm Adams."

Durant said, "You dirty, miserable bastard!" in a low voice and brought his fist down in a slashing punch at Adams' face. Adams turned his head through instinct and the blow caught him high on his right cheekbone. He and the chair crashed to the floor and he rolled once, stunned. He caught a glimpse of Durant's swinging foot and deflected the kick with his forearm. He scrambled to his feet, coming out of the shock, now, and Durant backed off a step. Adams walked to him and grabbed the right lapel of Durant's jacket in his left hand. He turned his thigh against the thrusting knee and drove his right hand savagely into Durant's face twice, then punched at the throat. The man collapsed, clutching at his collar with mewling, choking sounds.

Gordon said, "Christ!" Durant writhed on the floor, hands at the brutalized throat. His mouth was pulped red and his nose an unrecognizable smear. Gordon looked at Adams. "Never get angry with me! What do we do now?"

Adams held a hand to his eye. "Throw the son of a bitch out in the snow. Get him out of here." He walked from the bar into his apartment. He soaked a towel and bathed his face, bleeding now where Durant's ring had cut him. *A couple of stitches,* he thought, but it could wait until the morning.

His head throbbed and his face ached but the high anger in him abated. All right. The man had acted according to the pattern Ann had drawn of him. He'd acted, perhaps, as any man would when someone he had once loved had been destroyed.

Or maybe he'd just acted. It wasn't too difficult to accept the supposition that Durant had planned the scene, that his rage had been simulated, that the episode had been a contrivance which would depict Durant as a man embraced in the furies of grief.

Adams poured a heavy drink from a bottle in the cabinet and slumped on the sofa. He did not know what to think. Sorrow and confusion and anger and exhaustion had combined to cloud his mind to the point where the processes of thought were almost impossible. He drank half the whisky and Mamie knocked and came in from the kitchen.

She said, "More trouble, I hear." She examined his

face tenderly and said, "A doctor should look at that."

"In the morning," Adams said. "I'm beat." He finished his drink. "I'm for bed, Mamie."

"Do you want some warm milk?"

He shook his head. "If I could package the way I feel now I'd make a million in sleeping pills."

"I know it's a silly thing to say, but try not to worry. Everything will be all right."

There was love in her voice, and he smiled at her. "If you say so, Mamie."

He undressed and went to bed. He thought of the mess he was in, and then he remembered something else. He had troubles. But Ann was dead. He fell asleep thinking of her.

Chapter 15

IN THE MORNING he went down to West Fork and Dr. Brennan took two stitches in the skin above his cheekbone. He had a headache and a black eye to end all black eyes. When he went back up the hill he saw the state police car parked in the driveway. Lieutenant Mayo was in Adams' apartment, looking at a book. He stood up when Adams walked in.

"Mrs. Doyle asked me to wait in here."

"Sit down," Adams said. "Anything Mrs. Doyle tells you to do you'd better do." On the two other occasions he'd seen the man he had been distracted. Mayo was of medium height and slender. His eyes were dark, the mouth somehow untouched by cynicism. Adams said, "Like a drink?"

Mayo shook his head. "Office hours." Then he said, "I understand Durant was here last night."

"He made a visit."

"Dr. Brennan says his face is in bad shape."

"He walked in here and threw a sucker punch at me. What did he expect, drinks on the house?"

Mayo studied him for a moment. "You're supposed to be the artistic type."

"Sure. But I was raised in a steel town and I spent a couple of years walking forward and backward across

Korea. Maybe I'm a little queer, but I don't like to be punched in the mouth."

"Did you know he was up at Bald Mountain?"

Adams nodded. "He was pointed out to me the other day." He thought that was enough for now.

"Why didn't you tell us?"

"Everyone was so damned interested in me I didn't even think of it."

There was no expression in Mayo's eyes, but they were very steady. "Adams, what were you doing down in West Fork at four o'clock that morning?"

Adams didn't know what prompted him, but it was somehow clear that this was a moment for truth. "Mrs. Durant had dinner here with me. When things had slowed down I took her home. I thought the walk back up the hill would do me some good. At her place we had a few drinks and sat around talking. When I left her it was very close to four o'clock."

Mayo studied his hands for a long moment. "And she was alive."

"Yes." *Alive and almost asleep and smiling and beautiful.*

Mayo started to say something and changed his mind. He got up. "There'll be a lot more questions, Adams. Will you come over to Winslow if I give you a call?"

"Sure. I live here. I'm not running anywhere. The only objection I have to Winslow is Sands."

Mayo shrugged. "He likes you, too."

A half hour after Mayo left, Adams had his second and more direct contact with the press. One of the housegirls knocked on his door and said, "There's someone to see you, Mr. Adams." Her manner held a touch of awe.

He went into the lounge and two men and a woman sat there. They got up at his approach. One man said, "I'm Lawson of the Boston *Chronicle*. We'd like to know, Mr. Adams——"

Adams addressed each of them in turn. "No comment. No comment. No comment."

The woman said, "How long were you and Mrs. Durant lovers, Mr. Adams?"

Adams looked at her. Her hair was greasy under a tasteless felt hat, she was twenty pounds overweight and her tiny eyes were greedy. Adams said, "You must have been a horrible mess as a child, too. Get out of here.

Stay out." He turned away and went back to the apartment, feeling a little sick.

At noon Bill Tate called. "Hear you had some trouble."

"Of a minor nature. What's new?"

"We might have a thing here and there. You be home this evening? About eight?"

"If you say so."

"There'll be a fellow named Clark around. One of our friends. If he gets there before I do, you'll know who he is."

"Fine. Had some visitors. Lieutenant Mayo and some gentlemen and a lady of the press."

"Oh? How about Mayo?"

"He wanted to know what I was doing in town that night. I told him. Somehow it seemed the thing to do."

There was a brief silence. "All right. What else did he ask?"

"Nothing. Said he'd call me if he wants to see me."

"That sounds good enough. I'll be around later."

Adams ate a light lunch. He learned that Gordon had gone over to Bald Mountain, and wondered absently how the man had disposed of Durant the night before. That was someone he could do without, that Durant. At least Mayo was aware of him, now. He'd been due to come in for a little attention.

He thought about Mayo. There was no bluster in the man, no indication of personal animosity, as there had been in Sands. Theirs were different jobs, of course, and they went about them in different ways. He still didn't like Sands.

It was about two o'clock and Adams was in the bar checking the stock when he heard a woman say, "Hello." He felt the shock, knew he had made a mistake and looked up. But it was Helen, all right. Her red hair poked out from beneath a small hat; her cheeks had been touched by the cold. Her smile was provisional and said nothing.

Adams straightened from his stooped position. He said, "Hello. This is a surprise."

Helen shrugged. "I thought I'd see how things were going."

"Mamie called you."

"All right. Also I can read the newspapers. Also I have an old interest in this place and there should be someone around to run it while you're in jail." She looked at him. "That was a mistake. I'm sorry. I guess it isn't a moment for flippancy. What I meant was that maybe I can be of some help."

Adams nodded. "Sure. I understand." He was confused. He doubted that he had thought of Helen since this whole affair had started except when he and Tate had discussed how Sands would determine on a motive. Everything had been so immediate, events had moved so quickly, that he'd had no time to wonder how this would affect her. It had been selfish of him even if excusable.

He looked at her now. There had been no change in her loveliness. "What about the program?"

"I told them I didn't feel well, that I wanted some time off. They could understand that. They got Dorothy Foster to do it." Foster was a panel-show glamour girl. "She can't cook any better than I can."

"Half those viewers are going to come down with beriberi some day and then there'll be hell to pay. Where are your bags?"

"Out in what used to be our living room. What have you done with the place?"

He showed her through the house and he was somehow pleased that she liked what he had done. "Cute as a button," she said. "And you mean that Strick Lewis and Henny Taylor and their mobs come up here now and pay you?"

"Through the nose. They don't seem to mind."

"We should have put a collection box at the door years ago. We'd be millionaires." She looked at him. "What are you going to charge me?"

He took her into what was now his small apartment. "It's yours. I'll move my junk upstairs."

She shook her head. "No. I'm strictly a visitor. I'll take that big room on the west and be very happy. Besides, I want to see if I can learn to use that cute little stove."

"Don't try to cook anything on it. Have you seen Mamie?"

She nodded. "She heard the taxi drive up and came out." She took off her hat. "Buy me a drink. That train ride is a killer."

They went out into the empty bar and Adams made two drinks. He brought them to a table and Helen said, "All right. Tell me what this is all about."

"A woman was killed. She'd had dinner here with me and I took her home. Someone saw me in West Fork at four o'clock in the morning, the approximate time of the murder, and the police grabbed me."

She tasted her drink and looked at him. "Roll in the hay department?"

"No. Nothing as casual as that."

"Did she know about us?"

"There are no secrets in this town. Yes, of course."

And Adams wondered how you dealt with a situation like this. How did you explain to a woman who had been your wife for six years your relationship with another woman? He had an idea he was going to find out.

There was acid in Helen's voice. "You certainly didn't waste any time, did you?"

"What do you mean by that?"

"Just that one day you leave me and the next you're involved with someone else. You don't scar easily."

Adams knew a slow anger. "I asked you to come up here. You didn't want anything to do with it."

She looked up at him. "You knew we were through. That we'd been through for a long time."

"All right. The fact that you don't want me doesn't make me a social outcast. Neither does it mean I have to invest in a cowl. And I didn't ask you to come up here now. As a matter of fact, I don't know whether or not I want you here. Besides, you miss the point. The woman is dead."

She didn't speak for a moment, then she said, "Yes, the woman is dead. I'm truly sorry, Johnny. It's the last of that you'll hear from me." She took a deep breath and sipped her drink. "What use can I be? What can I do around here?"

His anger dissolved. "You can supervise Mamie in the kitchen." She grinned wryly. "No, there must be a lot of things. You'll get ideas for change, for decoration; things that would never occur to me."

"You've done all right. Really a nice job."

"I could never figure out why, but you're very good with figures. There's a surprising amount of bookkeeping attached to this enterprise and it's all a great mystery to me. You might take that over to start with. If this snow keeps up we're going to be busy and there's actually much more work than I can handle. People will phone for reservations, and then you're supposed to remember about the reservations. Stuff like that."

Helen finished her drink. "Okay, boss. You just devote your energies to getting out of this jam and I will take over the broom. All right?"

Adams said, "A good deal and thank you." For a moment he felt closer to her than he had in a year.

They had dinner with a surprised Gordon. He said, "This is fine! Who's minding the store in New York? How do we sell pots and pans and stoves with you up here?"

Helen told him of the arrangements that had been made. "And you don't seem to be earning that monumental salary, Mr. G."

"Even genius must rest occasionally. Besides, my boy is in a pickle and I have to hang around to see how things work out."

They finished dinner and Gordon went to his room and Helen thought she'd have an introductory look at the books.

Chapter 16

IT WAS JUST A LITTLE BEFORE EIGHT when a slender man in his thirties came into the bar and introduced himself to Adams as George Clark. Adams had just bought him a drink when Tate arrived. They all sat at a corner table and Tate said, "Well, George, how is everything over at Bald Mountain?"

"It seems to be quite a place." Clark's voice was even and unhurried. "Much hanky-panky once the skis come off. The bellhops and the maids are a little jaded by it all and a ten-dollar bill goes a long way. Item of interest: Sidney Durant was absent from his room at Pepper's Inn on the night of the fifteenth. The bed was not slept in. I haven't yet been able to find out where he was. Item: Phillip Gordon *did* spend the night of the fifteenth at Bald Mountain. In the company of a Miss Dolores Mendoza. He was observed leaving her room very close to five o'clock. It doesn't eliminate him, but from what I've seen of Miss Mendoza I doubt Gordon was at that moment in a mood for violence."

Tate asked, "What about your man in town here—Nelson?"

Clark frowned. "He's picked up a bit of this and that, but nothing very much. It takes a few days to know a town and you can't very well bribe the people to talk."

"What a waste of money that would be!" Adams said.

Clark continued. "I called New York an hour ago and they've done a pretty good job on Durant. He's very wealthy. He has never married again although there have been plenty of women. He has a reputation for arrogance, violence. It cost him a lot of money to clamp the hush on a brawl he had a year ago. He put a man's eye out."

Adams' hand went instinctively to the patch of adhesive on his cheek.

"That man interests me," Tate said. "Check him very carefully."

Clark nodded. "Of course. In New York they tell me Mrs. Durant had a very quiet background until she married Durant." He recited a list of facts Adams was familiar with. "They traveled and she obtained a divorce in Paris. We're still checking on her to see if there might have been . . ." he paused and Adams knew it was in deference to himself ". . . anyone else. That's about it so far."

"All right," Tate said. "We'll keep in touch."

"Have you had dinner?" Adams asked.

Clark shook his head. "Not yet."

Adams smiled. "You will." It was always a pleasure to introduce anyone to Mamie's cooking. "How about you, Bill?"

"I was a fool. I had mine." Then Tate said, *"There's* a lovely woman." His eyes were on the door, and Adams turned. Helen had just come back into the room.

He said, "I guess you're right." He felt very silly. "That's my wife."

Tate looked at him. "But I thought you told me . . ."

Adams nodded. "It was the truth. It still is. But she heard about this *brouhaha* and came climbing up the mountain."

Tate frowned. "It's going to complicate things."

"I can't see that it's going to help Sands. I believe it can be assumed she is not a shuddering idiot, therefore she reads. If she is not beside herself with rage but comes up here just to lend a hand, knowing what she knows, then it's apparent that she has a slightly objective view of the whole thing."

"I get your point, but it would have been nicer if she had kept her objectivity in New York. All right, she's here."

As a matter of fact, she was at the table. Adams introduced her to Clark and Tate, and they all sat down. "Bill is my lawyer."

She looked at Tate. "I don't imagine you approve of me being on the scene. Whoever is handling this on the other end would like to tie it tight with a triangular knot. Something about the other woman coming to me, et cetera, et cetera."

"Not about that."

"The woman thinks fast," Tate said.

"Not being a moron is nothing, really," Helen said. "But to set you at ease, Johnny and I have been on the verge of breaking it up for some time. As for my presence here, we're strictly chaperoned by our cook."

Tate nodded. "All right." He addressed Adams. "Since you talked with Mayo this morning he has undoubtedly talked with Sands. They'll be after you again very shortly and I imagine they won't have any trouble getting an arraignment for manslaughter, since you admit being on the scene."

"Maybe I was foolish," Adams said, "but I felt he knew it anyway."

"You're probably right. It would be difficult for them to prove premeditation, so they'll leave it at manslaughter. They can always raise the charge. So I talked with Ken Meadows at the bank and he says they'll go up to seventy-five thousand dolars on your property and its potential. I don't think the bail will be set that high, but it's always nice to have a cushion. Above seventy-five we'll have to go elsewhere."

And in the morning Mayo made another visit to the hotel. "Want to take a little ride?"

"To Winslow?"

Mayo nodded, and Adams said, "mind if I use the phone?"

Mayo said, "Go ahead," and Adams called Tate. "I'm being escorted to Winslow."

"I'll meet you there and drive you back."

Adams was putting on his coat when Helen came into the lounge. Adams introduced her to Mayo. The lieutenant said, "Nice to know you, Mrs. Adams. We knew you were here. Up for the skiing?"

Helen said, "Yes. It's a charming little village you have here." Adams watched her measure the man. "What are you going to do with him?"

"Nothing much. Just lock him up."

"Oh," she said. "Well, that's all right." She touched Adams on the shoulder. "I'll watch the pennies, Johnny."

In the state police car Mayo was silent for several minutes, then he said, "Your wife is quite an unusual woman."

Adams thought about it and said, "Yes." Then he asked, "Before you questioned me yesterday, did you already know I had visited Mrs. Durant that night?"

For a moment he thought Mayo wasn't going to answer, then the lieutenant said, "Yes. I can't think of any reason for not telling you. We checked your movements all during the day and you hadn't left the hotel. But your fingerprints were on that day's paper in the Durant apartment."

Adams nodded. His hunch had been correct. Lying to Mayo would have been a grave mistake.

Tate met them at the courthouse in Winslow. When they went up to his office Sands wore a badly fitting gray suit and a smirk. "So now it's starting to come out, eh, Adams? You were up in her apartment that night."

"Someone must have told you." There was about this man something that grated on Adams. There was a meanness in him, a smallness.

"And she screamed that she was going to your wife and you strangled her."

"No," Adams said. Were they going to go through all this again?

"You strangled her," Sands said, delighting in the words, mouthing them obscenely, "and then you raped her."

Adams contained himself. "No."

The smile faded from Sands face, then it appeared again. "I understand your wife is staying up at your hotel."

"That's right."

The grin was evil. "You manage not to run out of that stuff, don't you Adams?"

Adams leaned on the desk. "One thing I'm going to run out of very soon is patience, you slob. You just give me one more of your miserable gags and you'll be able to tack a simple assault charge onto whatever else you've got."

Sand's face became livid. In a moment he said, "Let's go. And keep your eye on him, Mayo. That man is dangerous.

Judge Kenyon listened to the district attorney, his fingers steepled. Sands said, "He admits being in the apartment at approximately the time the murder was committed, your honor. And he had plenty of motive." He pointed at Adams. "This man strangled Ann Durant because she threatened to go to his wife and tell her the whole sordid story. He was frightened, frantic. He had probably been planning such a move for days and acted at a time when he was sure he wouldn't be seen on the streets. But he was fooled."

Judge Kenyon coughed lightly. "I understand that Mrs. Adams is now resident at her husband's hotel in West Fork. This does not seem the normal reaction of an enraged woman but instead bespeaks a strong objectivity, to say the least."

"If I may interrupt, your honor," Tate said. "Mr. and Mrs. Adams have for some time been contemplating a separation. Mr. Adams told me this and his wife confirmed it."

The judge nodded. "It seems presumable that this decision was reached before Mr. Adams met Mrs. Durant. Mrs. Adams' attitude, her presence here, indicates that."

Sand was not finished. "Mr. Sidney Durant, the husband of the deceased, is staying at Bald Mountain. Mrs. Durant had dinner there with him one night. I suggest that a reconciliation was effected, that Adams was informed of this and strangled Mrs. Durant in a rage. He is capable of great violence, your honor. He assaulted Mr. Durant viciously only two days ago."

Adams felt the judge's eyes on his battered face. "Did Mr. Durant press charges?"

"Well, no, your honor. It seems——"

"It seems that Mr. Adams was somewhat assaulted, too."

"He even threatened me, your honor, not fifteen minutes ago."

Bill Tate said, "Your honor, Mr. Sands made a very insulting remark not at all pertinent to these proceedings. Mr. Adams objected."

Sands flushed but said. "Your honor, I'd like this man charged with first-degree murder."

Judge Kenyon peered at him. "Which of your stated motives do you prefer, Mr. Sands?" He shook his head. "There is no evidence of correspondence between Mr. Adams and Mrs. Durant that would bear out either of your theories, and apparently no one ever heard them discuss either subject. What you state as fact is mere conjecture. That Mr. Adams visited the apartment is significant of course, but it is my view that he can be held only as a material witness. Sufficiently high bail has already been posted." He peered over his spectacles. "We certainly would not like to lose Mr. Adams. And Mr. Sands, I will be perfectly willing to review any further evidence you might like to present in the future."

In the corridor, Adams and Tate met Mayo. The lieutenant stopped for them. He said to Adams, "I'm sure you would have volunteered the information by now if you had seen anyone on the street in West Fork at four o'clock that morning."

"I certainly would have," Adams said. "But I didn't see a soul." *Just walking in the snow, thinking of the loveliness he had left. . .*

Mayo nodded and started to walk away. Tate said, "Lieutenant, about this Durant. Does he account for the fact that he didn't sleep in his room at Pepper's Inn that night?"

Mayo looked at him. "So you have some people on the job? Everyone wants to get into the act?"

"A little pressure on Durant wouldn't displease me," Tate said. "He's been in tough scrapes before. He's fully capable of something like this."

"You know more about him that we do?"

"Maybe," Tate said, and gave Mayo the information Clark had dispensed the night before. He said, "As you can see, we're very anxious to help the authorities."

Mayo nodded. "Thank you. I'll see that you get a gold star on your report." He walked away.

Tate said, "He's a strange one. I don't figure him."

"I don't mind him. He seemes to have little curiosity,

a quality I greatly admire at the moment, when everyone else is being so positive."

It was just after one o'clock when they got back to West Fork, and Adams went in to see Ken Meadows at the bank. "It's all right," Meadows said when Adams thanked him. "We're posting nothing but your money, really."

The man's eyes were level and Adams could see in them no accusation, no trace of prejudgment. He said, "Well, I certainly appreciate this unusual sort of service. You've made yourself a very permanent client."

"I certainly hope we can keep him," Meadows said, and there was the trace of a grin at one corner of his mouth. Adams looked at him in surprise, then laughed and went out.

Chapter 17

AT COOLEY'S, most of the luncheon customers had left and Mary was washing glasses behind the bar. She looked tired. Troubled, Adams thought. And usually she was so serene. Her voice was almost anxious. "Anything new, Johnny?"

He shook his head and something passed through her eyes but he did not know what it was. "I heard that Helen's up at the hotel."

"Arrived yesterday. She'll be down to see you. As a matter of fact, I have to call in a few minutes and tell her to come get me."

Mary looked at him. "She's a good girl, Johnny, to be coming up here now. It couldn't have been easy for her."

"I know," Adams said. He had thought about that.

The tall woman said, "It doesn't look very good, does it, Johnny?"

That fact had been made increasingly clear to Adams during the last several days. Unless something turned up on Durant, the efforts of the investigators would be even more strongly centered on himself. Purely circumstantial evidence had condemned men before him. He said, "No, not very good." Then he smiled at Mary. "A bourbon would help, though."

She started to say something, then made the drink.

She shook her head. "It's all a shame. A sorry shame."

Cooley came in from the kitchen, then. Mary walked from behind the bar and said. "Tell Helen I was asking for her. And that I'm sorry."

Adams said, "I will, Mary." Then he said, "Hello, Joe."

Cooley merely nodded, and Adams watched him make a huge whisky sour. He took several long swallows from the mixing glass, then set it on the bar. "Should be good for what ails me." His eyes were bloodshot. "A rough night." He lit a cigarette. "How does it go? What are they doing to you, boy?"

"Nothing much."

"Not like being at a clambake though, eh?"

"No marked similarity."

"You need that money? That couple of thousand I mentioned?"

Adams shook his head. "No thanks, Joe. They seem to figure I've anted up enough."

"I understand that the former husband was over at Bald Mountain. They talked to him yet?"

"They don't confide in me very much, but I would suppose so." And if they had talked to him, Adams wondered, what had they found out?

Cooley finished his drink and started making another. Adams went to the phone and called the hotel. Helen would come down in about ten minutes. He went back to the table and his drink.

Cooley said, "It's hard to believe that four or five days could make such a difference. You were all goosed up about opening your place and Miz Durant was happy. And alive."

"Things have changed," Adams agreed.

"Just can't seem to get it into my head," Cooley said. "I'll always remember her just as she looked the day she died, pretty as hell and that nice smile always workin'."

Adams nodded. Vibrant from a day on the hill, her eyes bright and filled with laughter, her skin glowing from the weather and the exercise. And later, fragrantly sleepy.

Cooley drank as if in memoriam. Then he said, "That Sands isn't the most pleasant guy in the world, from what I hear."

"I guess he's just doing his job. I can't say I'm fond of him." And Adams again considered the possible fruits of the official questioning of Durant, which must have taken place by now. Certainly, in his brief encounter with the man Durant had plainly demonstrated that he was capable of the most marked violence. If he had still been in love with Ann, if he had succeeded in deluding himself that she was still one of his possessions, and somehow learned of her relationship with Adams, it was not unthinkable that he had come over in the night and killed her.

He had another drink and Joe said, "I hear Helen came up."

"That's right. Yesterday."

Cooley shook his head. "The good ones are hard to believe. No kiyoodle in them. They stay with it."

It was the truth. Adams knew plenty of women who would not have lifted a finger, certainly never under the peculiar circumstances. But then Helen had never been frightened of trouble, had never panicked at the tough situations they had encountered. It was too bad they hadn't made it, that he had lacked whatever it was Helen needed.

She came in the door, then, saw him and walked to the table. She stopped at the bar and shook hands with Cooley. "Good to see you, Joe."

"Nice to have you back, Helen. Missed you. Something to drink?"

"A bourbon on the rocks sounds like this time of day."

"Pleasure of the house," Cooley said. "We're tryin' to drum up business."

She sat next to Adams and said, "Well, how did the Boy Allies do with the Gestapo?"

"They have no one else to aim at," Adams said. "If it goes on like this I'm the only target for tonight. I can't blame them, but I can't honestly say I like it."

"What about this Durant character? Have they put the rubber hoses to him yet?"

"I don't know. But I'd like to."

Cooley brought Helen's drink to the table. "I'm a hell of a reception party. About the only thing I can think of is what my uncle used to say: When you're all the way down, there's no place to go but up."

"You just keep your lousy proverbing relatives to yourself," Adams said. "I've had about enough of this rustic wisdom. Look where it's got me."

"All right," Cooley said. He went back and sipped at his drink.

"Mary was asking for you, a few minutes ago."

"It'll be nice to see her. But how about you? What do you do now?"

Adams shrugged. "There'll probably be a meeting of the board of strategy at the hotel tonight. Unless the gendarmes pick me up before then, I guess I'm not very busy."

"All right. How about riding me over to Bald Mountain? A couple of hours on the hill wouldn't do either of us any harm."

It sounded like a good idea. Adams said, "Finish your drink." In a few moments they left and he told Joe, "See you later."

They put in two hours of enjoyable work before the oncoming darkness made them quit. They had picked up Gordon at the base of one of the lifts and they all had a drink together at Pepper's.

"Damnedest week end I've ever had," Gordon said, "outside of one I spent in Guadalcanal."

Adams said nothing. It was shocking to think that only a few days ago he had been here with Ann.

A rich, low voice said, "Pheeleep, my darling! Where were you hiding from Dolores? You are a bad, bad boy!"

Adams turned. Standing at the table was a tall woman, slim but magnificently rounded, wearing a gray ski outfit that must have been poured on her. Her eyes were deep and dark, her mouth wide and full and pouting, now. She was beautiful.

Gordon got to his feet. "Ah, the Light of the Central American Republics! How have you ever been?"

"You have desert me!" the woman moaned quietly. "You have make of me a cast-off. I am desoleet!"

Gordon made the introductions. Adams watched Dolores eye Helen, and apparently sensing this was no rival, she touched Helen's face. "But you are beeyootiful! Even in my country they would fight the *duello* ovare a woman like you."

Gordon said, "Sit down, Dolly. And please stop that Latin lunacy. They never raised you to speak like that in Chicago."

The woman sat down, took a cigarette from a package, and Adams lighted it for her. She said, "Phil Gordon, you're a bastard. Where the hell have you been? And how can I learn to act if I don't practice?"

"I've been over here skiing for the last few days. I haven't seen you on the hill."

The woman looked at Gordon and her smile was slow and langorous. "Skiing! After all, Phil!" Her tone became intimate. "Now, the other night, darling . . ."

Gordon coughed. "What I've always liked is a little neon-lighted privacy. You have a one-track mind. Don't you ever think of anything else? Let there be a change of subject. How is your aunt?"

The girl grinned at him. "Still running that house."

They had an enjoyable hour. Adams and his wife left Gordon with the girl. On their way home Helen said, "She's beautiful. And a lot of fun."

"She's about the most pleasant alibi a man could possibly have."

"Alibi?"

Adams told her of the check on Gordon's activities.

She stared at him. "You don't mean you'd suspect Phil?"

"Why not? This is the season of suspicion, the winter of wondering. He knew Ann Durant years ago. I feel like a fifth-rate bastard, but your viewpoint changes when you see them approaching with that noose."

Helen shuddered. "I wish things weren't like this. I wish they were the way they had been."

And Adams wondered what she meant by that.

When they got back to the hotel there was a message to call Tate. The lawyer said that he and Clark would be over about eight, if that was all right. Adams said it was fine with him. He wondered what they might have turned up.

He was busy for a few hours. People who had jumped the week-end gun started arriving. He was aware of their stares, but only a few whom he knew well patted him on the shoulder and said they were sorry to hear about the trouble. He was forced to conclude bitterly that a little murder here and there didn't do business any harm.

It was a bit after eight when Tate and Clark showed up, and there was another young man with them whom Tate introduced as Harry Nelson. They again sat at a corner table. Clark said, "First of all, about Durant. I'm afraid he's out. He spent the night in a cabin over at Pine Lodge. With a Miss Mary Knowles."

Adams said, "Well, I'll be damned." Mary Knowles was the new, bright star of a hit New York musical.

"It cost me a twenty to find out. Durant is also a heavy backer of her show, the New York people say. She was back in New York by late Monday afternoon, before the body was discovered, and I will bet she is sweating small bullets at this point."

Tate fingered his lip. "Not good. He's certainly told the police that by now and they've checked. It puts us up that creek again."

"I've found nothing else helpful," Clark said. "The New York office turned up a lot of negligible information on Durant and Gordon. None of it helps us at all. We'll have to start figuring this thing from a different angle." Adams felt his glance and was aware of the conjecture it contained. It would be fine if his own club started rooting against him.

Tate said to the other man, "What did you come up with, Harry?"

Nelson said, "These small towns always amaze me." He consulted some notes. "Mr. Fowler, the high school principal, with a wife and three children, is carrying on a very torrid affair with Miss Simmons, the librarian. This has been going on for three years. They are frequent guests at a motel over in Hillsboro."

"Intriguing." Tate said. "Everyone knows that."

"And that Mr. Barberry, the greengrocer, dutifully supports his two illegitimate children by a waitress in High Falls? That Dr. Brennan's wife has no sister in Boston, whom she is supposed to visit for about a week every month? That Mrs. Smith's handsome son has a dishonorable discharge from the Army, where he was barely acquitted of rape? And why not suspect him, by the way, since he was supposed to have been visiting a cousin in Concord that night, a fact I haven't been able to confirm? He frequently sat with Mrs. Durant, talking, when she went to Mrs. Smith's to eat. He was heard to quarrel with his mother about this. Many other items of interest."

"There are skeletons here and there," Tate admitted. "Anything germane to the issue?"

Nelson frowned. "The Smith son could stand a bit of looking into. Big, handsome, surly." Then he said, "And the town has another nightwalker, besides Mr. Adams. Joe Cooley has been seen on the streets after midnight, on many occasions."

"So he closes late," Adams said. "He goes for a walk. I know that feeling."

"Loud quarrels in the household, too," Nelson said. "Mrs. Cooley didn't put in a public appearance for three days, about a month ago. When she did, there were indications of bruises on her face."

"Everybody quarrels, I guess," Tate said. "When Joe gets a load on he's been known to be a little physical. I don't suppose Mary Cooley is the only woman in this town to have been slapped in the face."

It surprised Adams that the Cooleys might have strong differences, but then he had never thought much about it. And he did remember without pride an occasion when, in anger and frustration, he had slapped Helen. No one was beyond stupidity, it seemed.

Tate said, "All right. Check Harold Smith's story. With Durant and Gordon out of the picture he's about all we have left."

"I'll go to Concord tomorrow," Clark said. "You get me names and places, Harry." Nelson nodded.

"We might as well have a drink," Adams said, "to celebrate nothing at all." He turned to Tate. "So?"

"So we keep punching. Something has to turn up. The woman didn't throttle herself." Then Tate said, "In the meantime, we get very damn busy working out a defense."

Adams said slowly, "It won't be easy."

Tate shook his head. "No, it won't be easy."

Adams felt the first breath of panic, then. The sequence of events in the months ahead were strangely clear to him. In the years ahead. If there were to be years. He fought down the fear. He said, "Something will turn up." The lack of conviction in his voice echoed back at him.

Tate punched him on the arm. "*You* can't stop believing that."

Adams looked at him and grinned. He was over the jitters. He said, "I won't, William."

Chapter 18

IT WAS WELL AFTER NINE when the three men left. Adams and Helen and the returned Gordon sat at a table and he gave them the gist of what had been discussed.

"All right," Gordon said with finality. "The lawyers come up from New York tomorrow. Your boy might be bright enough, but it looks very much as if he could use a little help, about now. I'm sure he won't object."

Adams thought about it. "I guess he wouldn't. I won't."

Helen said, "What happens now?"

Adams could guess. "With everyone else out of the way, I don't think my friend Mr. Sands will have any trouble getting an indictment against me for manslaughter. From there on it's up to Bill Tate, may he be a genius."

A couple of late guests arrived and Adams took care of them. When he returned to the bar Gordon had gone to his room.

Helen said, "It's not an exciting thought, but would you like to play some chess? Or gin?"

He shook his head. There was a restlessness on him, the feeling an animal must have when it finds something wrong with familiar surroundings and is wary of a trap. Something had been annoying him for the past hour, some shadowy fact that had been nibbling at a corner of his mind and which he could not identify. A name forgotten, a date temporarily lost, the evasive title of a book? Something that had been said? Something he had seen? He couldn't tell. He didn't even know whether or not the small, insistent, unintelligible whisper was pertinent to the occasion.

He said, "I think I'll walk into town. I've got the willies and a walk might shake them. Maybe if I hiked around, the way I did that night, I might see something, or be reminded of something, that would help."

"Want me to come?"

He said, "No, thanks. I won't be very long. Probably stop at Cooley's for a drink, if he's still open."

Helen's grin was gentle. "Don't get locked up."

"I'll try to be careful."

The moon was high and almost full, and the tree shadows were heavy on the snow. There was no wind, but the cold was formidable and Adams pulled tight the string of the fur-lined hood on his jacket. He went over the events of the day, the conversation of the evening, and in none of it could he find any encouragement. Ann's death had been a terrible, apparently pointless thing. That he might be found guilty of her murder would complete the senselessness of the entire episode. And he knew very well, now, that in the absence of any other suspect his conviction would be almost assured.

At half past ten, the streets of West Fork were deserted and the town was seemingly asleep. He traced in reverse the route he had taken that night he had left Ann. It was, in fact, the only logical course. North on Main to the library, and then west on Elm. He stood in front of the house for a moment, then crossed the street and looked at it from the gate to the lumberyard. The windows of the apartment gazed blankly at the night, telling him nothing, reminding him of nothing. He was sure he had not seen anyone, that early morning. There might have been someone about, but he had not thought it likely he would meet anyone and had not been looking for anyone. Things had been very different, that night.

He went back to Main and turned north again toward Cooley's. He wondered if Mrs. Greer and Miss Alice Stanton had seen him tonight. They would certainly make a tale of it tomorrow.

There was a light in Cooley's but when he tried the door it was locked. He looked in and saw Joe sitting at a table. Adams knocked, watched Cooley peer down the long room, then get up and come to the door. He opened it for Adams, locked it again when he was inside. "Just happened to see it was you," he said. "Nobody around now except someone might happen to drive through. Waste of time, stayin' open." His speech was a bit slurred, and as he walked before Adams to the table, his gait was too deliberate. "You walk down? I didn't see any car."

"Yeah, I walked," Adams said.

"Cold enough to freeze that brass monkey. How about a toddy?"

"It sounds good," Adams said. He took off his jacket

and Cooley went behind the bar, made the drink, then poured boiling water from a Silex pitcher on an electric hot plate. He brought it to the table. "How come you don't stay up at the hotel and drink your own whisky on a night like this?"

"Restless," Adams said. "Thought I'd visit the metropolis, look at all the bright lights."

Cooley snorted. "Dead. On some Saturday nights it's worthwhile staying open until twelve. During the week you might just as well go to bed at ten." He was drinking whisky in a tall glass. He took a heavy swallow. "I've been tryin' to get out of this town since I was ten years old. Never made it, except for a couple of years in the Navy. Should have stayed in."

"You get sick of the big towns, too," Adams said. "I like this one."

Cooley looked at him. "You like it. Sure. You can afford to like it. And you can get out when you like. I'm stuck here."

Adams said, "It looks a little as if I'm stuck here too."

Cooley said, "Hell, I forgot about that." He finished his drink, went behind the bar and poured himself another. Adams thought absently that Cooley was going to feel horrible again tomorrow, at this rate.

"It's a loused-up town," the big man said. "It's full of little dirt and big gossip. It's a hard-luck town. Look what happened to you. Look what happened to Miz Durant."

"She liked the town," Adams said.

"Sure. It treated her fine." Cooley drank. Someone tried the front door and Cooley said without turning his head, "Closed. The hell with you."

Something started to click in Adams' mind, the shapeless thing that had been gnawing at him for hours was beginning to take some sort of form. He could not recognize it yet and he was almost afraid to try, now.

"With you people it's different," Cooley said. "You can come here when you want, leave when you please. You drift up here for the snow and think the country and the people are just for your benefit." Adams had seldom seen Joe so drunk before, and those other occasions had been happy ones.

"You and your friends come in here as if you were slumming. Some of the women treat me as if they'd been expecting me to wear a coonskin cap and spit on the floor. Money's a joke to you. Buy a house! Buy a mountain! What the hell, it's only money. And I scrape away here for years. For what? For nothing."

"It wasn't that way at all, Joe."

"Maybe not between you and me. Maybe."

And then the thing that had been tapping at the entrance of Adams' mind was suddenly inside, big and terrible. He remembered, now. He said, "Oh, no!"

Cooley looked at him. "What?"

Cooley had said at noon, *"I'll always remember her just as she looked the day she died."* And Cooley hadn't seen her the day she died! Ann had told Adams that she had gone to Bald Mountain early, immediately after breakfast. She had come straight to the hotel when she left the hill. Adams had been with her from then on. But perhaps she had met Joe in town in the morning.

Adams said, "When did you see Ann Durant on Sunday, Joe?"

"What are you talking about?"

"I just asked when you had seen her."

"She came in here in the afternoon for a drink. We shot the breeze."

Adams shook his head, almost not believing this himself. "She wasn't in here, Joe. She was over in Bald Mountain all day and then she came to my place. When did you see her, Joe?"

"I told you," Cooley said. His face was set in stubborn lines. "In here, in the afternoon." He tasted his drink almost with caution.

"You're lying, Joe. When did you see her? It wasn't during the day. Was it when I left her, early in the morning? Did you go up there, Joe?" He was speaking of unreality, of the impossible he was afraid had occurred.

Cooley looked at him, the eyes sobering. "You're crazy, Adams."

Adams shook his head. "No. You must have waited until I had gone, and then you went up to see her. She would have known your voice. She would have let you in."

Cooley lit a cigarette and tasted his drink. "You're tryin' a little too hard to get off that hook, Adams. I don't think you did it. You don't shape up like that kind of a guy. But don't try to shove it off on me." He took a long swallow of the drink.

"I'm just asking you one thing. Where did you see her that day if you didn't go up there? You couldn't have seen her, Joe. She wasn't in here."

Cooley stared at him, the eyes clouding slightly as if a memory had passed over them. Over the man's shoulder Adams saw Mary Cooley standing on the stairs that led up to the apartment. Cooley was unaware of her.

He was silent for a long moment, then he said, as if this thing had been buried within him for a long time and had to come out, "It gets damned cold standing in that lousy lumberyard across the street from her place. Nights when I closed I'd stand back there and just watch her windows. Nights when you were there, Adams. Nights when you weren't." He drank. "Sure, I saw you bring her home that night. She got out of the car and the street light hit her face and I wondered what was making her so happy. Something I didn't have for her. She never looked like that at me."

Adams said, "Joe . . ."

Cooley talked, his eyes fixed on the wall someplace in back of Adams, on some point in the past. "I almost knew her as well as you did, Adams. One night she was in here drinking and I took her home and kissed her. That was all she would have. Maybe if you hadn't come along . . ." His eyes touched Adams. "But it wasn't anything to do with you, Adams. Much. It's just this—how many women are there around like that? How many for me? And I loved her. Did you? Would you freeze your brains out night after night, standing in the snow for hours just to get a look at her? Would you, Adams?"

Adams was afraid to think. "Joe, you didn't . . ."

The big shoulders moved. "I don't know. I saw the two of you go in and I couldn't stand it another time. I came back here and did myself some real drinking. Maybe I went out again. Maybe I went up there and——" He shrugged and drank again. "Who knows what a man would do for a woman like that? When he thought about her the way I did, I mean. You like your whisky, Adams. You ever black out? Wake up in the morning and the car's in the garage and you wonder how the hell you drove fifty miles without remembering any of it?"

"That's different, Joe." Adams was filled with pity and

something a little like horror. "Feeling about her the way you did, you wouldn't go up there and . . ."

Cooley finished his drink and poured another. "I just don't know, Adams. I'd thought of it, I guess. Way in the back of my head someplace. I might have done it. There's a chance."

Someone stepped out of the darkened kitchen. Lieutenant Mayo seemed even slimmer in civilian clothes. He said, "Yes, there's a chance, Joe."

Cooley just stared at him, the handsome flushed face going slack. He said, "What are you doing here?"

"I went up to see Adams, and his wife told me he'd probably be down here. I saw you talking and I tried the front door and it was locked. The back door was open."

Mary Cooley came down the stairs. She looked at the three men and said nothing.

"What did you want to see me about?" Adams asked.

"We're pretty busy people," Mayo said. "We're not as easily satisfied as Mr. Sands. We've been making door to door inquiries in Mrs. Durant's immediate neighborhood. We found another woman with curiosity and insomnia. Mrs. Tolson. She lives just across the street from the apartment. She'd been sick and we weren't able to talk with her until this afternoon." He lit a cigarette. Cooley had not moved. "Mrs. Tolson saw you leave the Durant apartment early on the mornings of November fifteenth, eighteenth, twenty-second and twenty-sixth, Adams. We even have the hours.

Adams said, "So?"

"Mrs. Tolson also saw Joe Cooley standing in the lumberyard practically every night for the last two months. I went up to the hotel to ask you if Mrs. Durant ever mentioned that Cooley had annoyed her. That was all I wanted of you." He turned. "I guess you'd better get a coat, Joe. Some things I'd like to ask you."

Cooley nodded heavily and got up. He started to say something to Adams, then turned away. He took a heavy coat from a hook on the wall and put it on. He went up to his wife, stood before her for a moment, then shook his head. He went through the kitchen in front of Mayo. Adams listened and heard the door close behind them.

He was numbed. And somehow unbelieving. He poured whisky with a shaking hand and brought the glass to Mary.

She shook her head and Adams said, "He didn't do it, Mary."

Her voice was flat. "I don't know. It's something you don't know about. Even he doesn't know."

"He couldn't have done it. He's not that sort of a man." Adams spoke more from hope than from conviction. This was Joe Cooley they were talking about. His friend. A gentle, drinking man.

Mary said evenly, her eyes dead in her white face: "You think Ann Durant was the first? Or the second or third? You think some of these friends you brought up here didn't encourage him? He's a handsome man with strong appetites." She seemed to Adams to be resigned.

"You knew all the time?"

"I guessed," the tall woman said. "Oh, God, how I didn't want to know! But I guessed. Going down through the alley so that Mrs. Greer wouldn't see him, then walking behind Simpson's to the lumberyard. Night after night. But he forgot about Mrs. Tolson. That miserable old woman."

Adams felt lost. "Well, look. I didn't do it, and I'm sure Joe didn't do it."

She faced him, her anger cold. "Do you think I care about you when he's concerned? Do you think I care what happens to you?" She turned, her eyes streaming silent tears, and slowly climbed the stairs to the apartment.

Adams stared after her for a moment, then drank the whisky in the glass he held. It almost sickened him. He got his coat and left through the darkened kitchen. He went along the side of the building to Main Street and saw his car at the curb. Helen was at the wheel. She moved over and he got in. He sat there in silence for a moment, trying to digest what had happened.

Helen said, "I saw Joe Cooley leave with Mayo. What does that mean?"

Adams told her, the whole thing becoming more incredible as he spoke. He said, "Joe didn't do it."

Helen said softly, "How do you know?"

"Just as I know I didn't do it. Hell, it doesn't figure. He isn't the sort of person to do it."

"Someone did it."

He nodded. "All right. It might have been Joe, the way he felt. It's possible. But I don't believe it."

"So what do we do now?"

Adams was tired to his core. "Nothing. Have a drink. Try to sleep. Wait."

Chapter 19

FRIDAY PASSED QUICKLY ENOUGH. Adams went into town at ten o'clock and saw Mary Cooley. She said, "Joe just called from Winslow." There was no trace of her agitation of the night before. "They're holding him in fifty thousand dollars bail. A material witness."

"We're just men of no distinction. Can you raise the money?"

She frowned. "I'm not sure. The bank said I could have half of it on this place. I guess I can go to a bondsman for the rest. If they have bondsmen over at Winslow."

Adams said, "The hell with that." He got Ken Meadows on the phone. "Ken, am I good for another twenty-five thousand?" He was remembering Cooley's offer.

"Buying a steak?"

Adams explained, and Meadows said, "Come pick it up."

Adams went back to Mary. "The rest is at the bank. Pick it up when you get yours."

Mary's face was expressionless. "Don't think I'm being bitchy, but it will have to wait for the afternoon. I'm getting lunch ready now. And its not going to kill me if Joe Cooley sits in a cell for a few hours."

"You want me to go?"

She looked at him. "Maybe you'd better. You and he seem to have quite a few things in common. Or maybe you'd rather send Helen over."

"All right," Adams said. "*Touché* for your side. You call Meadows and tell him I'll be over."

When he arrived at the bank Meadows had the checks ready for him. "If this keeps up I can see where we'll have to start a messenger service to Winslow."

Adams called Helen, told her what he was doing.

"You're something of a clobberhead," she said. "Why don't you leave him there? He wasn't very prompt with the information that he was hanging around the same corner, that night."

"You run the hotel. I'll manage the jail breaks."

On the ride to Winslow he pondered the possibility that Joe had committed the murder, and a strong voice within himself argued that such had not been the case. True that Joe might be an unfaithful husband, but the execution chambers of the nation would indeed be busy places if murder were to be the result of every infidelity. True that he said he had loved Ann. How strong that emotion had been Adams had no way of knowing, but he had an idea there were more powerful passions than an adult unconsummated desire. Since confessedly there had never been anything between Ann and Cooley but a drinking kiss, Adams doubted that the man's feelings could be murderously proprietary. And what made more sense to him than anything else was his unthinking conviction that Cooley could not have done the killing.

At Winslow, Adams found the court clerk without difficulty and presented the checks. The man said in a flat voice, "Guess you're our best customer."

"It's the price that intrigues me," Adams told him. "I always liked a place that has a set price. You can be sure you're not being gypped. I never did like these joints that go for thirty-five thousand one day and seventy thousand the next."

"We try to be reasonable," the man said, and signed some papers.

In a few minutes Cooley came into the room, accompanied by a guard. He looked like death warmed over. He said, "Mary didn't come?"

"She was busy with a pot roast. She thought you might like it here. It seems to me that we all might just as well move to Winslow."

A policeman came in and returned to Cooley a wallet and a key ring. "Hear you're leaving us."

Cooley fixed a horrible smile on his face. "Please don't feel bad about it. The accommodations were wonderful. It's just that I don't *like* you bastards."

They went out into the snow-magnified sunlight and Adams said, "You forgot to tell them you could do another stretch like that standing on your hands. Don't you ever go to the movies?"

"What are you doing here?"

"I didn't like it in there either. I figured you wouldn't. I just took a short ride to get some air."

Cooley looked at him for a long moment. "Okay. What I could use right now is a drink."

Adams pointed to a place across the street. "Anything wrong with that?" Cooley shook his head and they walked toward the bar. Adams said, "Glad to have you aboard the MWC."

"What?"

"I thought you were old Navy. The Material Witness Club. Restricted membership. There aren't many of the old crowd left."

"You're a little punchy," was Cooley's opinion. "Maybe that's why I always liked you."

The bar was warm and empty. They chose a table in the back and ordered double whisky sours. They took the first drink and Cooley gestured toward the courthouse across the street.

"Those people can be very disagreeable."

"I find them charming. Particularly their Mr. Sands."

Cooley muttered an obscenity. "I took a swing at him but I was so drunk I missed. One day I will catch up with that skinny-butted punk when he is without guards. It will probably cost me a worthwhile ten days in the can."

They finished the drink and Adams called for refills. When they came, he said, "You going to be able to square things with Mary, after last night?"

"She got it all?"

"I'm afraid she did. She heard us talking and came downstairs. You didn't see her."

Cooley frowned. "Maybe I'll be able to make it with the kid. Maybe. I'm a slob, and it seems to me that once a slob always a slob. I could be wrong. A guy could grow out of it if he's lucky."

Adams tried to think of something to say to that. He rummaged around in his philosophic file and found nothing suitable. He settled for, "Let's drink to that."

They drank and ordered another. Cooley said, "And where the hell did Mary raise fifty thousand dollars? I haven't got anything like that and the place has a mortgage half that big. Besides, after what you tell me she heard last night, I don't figure why she should send me half a dollar."

Adams said, "Well, the bank got it up. She called Meadows." It was truthful enough.

"I always have a hell of a time getting a dime out of him," Cooley said. "He must be drunk."

"We'll drink to that," Adams said. They had four sours apiece before they turned off the lemon juice. Whisky and water was quicker and neater. Adams felt strangely fine. He was as strongly convinced of Cooley's innocence as he was certain of his own. That he himself remained the primary suspect was hardly shocking. He'd been wearing the guise for days.

They drank methodically, and at one point Adams was aware of someone saying, "We'd better take it easy. It's real early in the afternoon."

And someone else said, "That's where we got them, boy. It's still real early."

Adams was aware of a toast to West Fork, of a toast to New York City, a toast to New York State and another to New Hampshire. They drank several poxes to Sands. One of them wept slightly.

Chapter 20

ADAMS AWAKENED to a sense of violence. He was being strenuously shaken and his face was being slapped. He opened his eyes and was amazed to see that Helen was the sole source of all the trouble. He sat up and gazed around. He was in his own bed and Helen stood beside it. In the background he vaguely discerned dim shapes he succeeded in identifying as Bill Tate and Clark, the investigator. His head ached horribly. He said the first thing that came to mind.

"I want a drink."

"You need it," Helen said. "Like a sharp stick in the eye. What you get is this." She handed him a cup of black coffee. It was steaming. She told him, "Drink that and wake up. These gentlemen have something of importance to tell you. Get alive, Adams."

The coffee was too hot to drink. He set it on the night table and blessedly there was a pack of cigarettes there. He lighted one and his eyes began to focus.

"How did I get here?"

"That I wouldn't attempt to imagine. Your miracle rating is very high, boy. Your car is outside and in one piece."

He tried the coffee. It was scalding but it broke the fog. He said to Tate, "William, what's new?"

"Can you hear?"

"Get you loud and clear."

"Clark just got back from Concord. The cousin young Howard Smith was supposedly visiting last Sunday night was not in Concord last Sunday night. He was in New York."

Adams stared at him for a moment. "Please repeat."

"This kid is lying for some reason, and it might be the big reason. He was never in Concord that night, as far as Clark could find out. He checked hotels and motels. No Howard Smith. Hell, even if a man named Smith wanted to sign a register with a phony name he'd have to use Smith. Where was he?"

Adams smoked for a moment, took another drink of the coffee. Young Smith. He had never seen him, but thinking of his prim mother it was difficult to envision a violent child. But the field was narrowing down.

"I don't know where he was. Let's go and ask him." He got off the bed. "A shower is indicated, if you'll wait. I won't be long."

The shower brought him back to life and he dressed in fresh clothes. He went out and joined the rest and Helen had another cup of coffee for him. He poured a shot of whisky into it and tasted it. He thought he might well live. He said, "Well, how do we go about this?"

Tate answered. "Nelson knows the young gentleman's habits and is watching him now. It's going on ten o'clock. He will be in Teddy Haynes's bowling alleys. It's almost ritual for a Friday night. Clark goes in and speaks to him. Clark can assume a manner. It will assure anyone that if he is not the world's chief chief of police, he ought to be. Smith comes out and gets into the car and we talk to him. We hope."

"He'll know me," Adams said.

"And me. I'm representing you, as everyone is aware, but Inspector Clark has turned up a new angle and has asked us to come along."

Adams thought about it. "How about calling Lieutenant Mayo and getting him into the party? He has just a little more authority than we do."

"I thought about it," Tate said. "He'd probably tell us to keep our noses out of this, that Smith couldn't possibly be involved. I doubt they were interested enough in this stellar example of America's fighting youth to bother with him."

Adams put on a jacket and heavy coat. "Let us go and be counselors to the young." He turned to Helen. "If by any chance Mayo should stop by, tell him I've gone skiing."

She looked at him. "Don't take a real fall. You can't stand many more."

They rode in Tate's car into the village, Clark driving. Haynes's place was a gathering point for several towns in the vicinity, particularly on Friday and Saturday nights. There were eight alleys and they were always busy. Clark parked across the street from the place and Tate said, "I hope you can make it stick."

"I've done it with pros. When I bring him back here, you just let me do most of the talking." He went over into Haynes's.

Adams asked, "What do you think this will amount to?"

"We're looking for a needle," Tate reminded him. "It's a big haystack. You haven't got a thing to lose. Be patient."

"A little more of this and I'll be *a* patient."

"What were you and Joe Cooley trying to prove this afternoon?"

Adams considered the question. "I suppose just that a couple of guys who have known each other a fairly long time can have a drink together."

"You don't think Cooley did it."

Adams shook his head. "I don't think there's a chance. But what of this Durant character? There's nothing on him at all?"

"Nothing except what I've told you. Sands and Mayo have had him on the grill and I understand they checked with the Knowles girl, through the New York police. Their story works out. There's not even any reason for it to hit the papers, in view of what it would do to the girl."

"It's nice to know that everyone else in the state is in the clear but me. I feel like the only private in the army."

"Here comes Inspector Clark with what might be our out. Take it easy."

Adams eyed the figure crossing the street beside Clark. Henry Smith was a tall, heavy young man. In the street light his face was fleshy, the mouth sullen, his manner reluctant. He and Clark got into the front seat. Young Smith's voice was surprisingly thin and reedy.

"What's this all about, Inspector?"

"I'd just like to ask you a few questions," Clark said. "It won't take long. Where were you last Sunday night?"

Young Smith turned and looked into the rear seat. "What are they doing here?" he wanted to know. Then he said, "Mr. Tate! And that Adams! What the hell is all this?"

"I had to stop by to see Mr. Tate and Mr. Adams and they thought they might come along. But answer my question. Last Sunday night."

Young Smith was silent for a moment. "If you're going to do any questioning, I don't see why these people have to be around. Why don't we go to the police station? Or over to Winslow?"

Clark nodded. "You have a point there." He started the motor. "We'll go to Winslow."

Smith said suddenly, "Wait! I guess this might be all right." He lighted a cigarette. "Sunday night. Hell, that was the night I went over to Concord. Stayed with my cousin, Jim Fowler."

"No," Clark said. "You weren't in Concord on Sunday night."

"The hell I wasn't. You just ask old Jim. I was with him all night."

"We asked old Jim. Old Jim happened to be in New York for the week end. He didn't get back until Monday. So you sure weren't with old Jim."

Smith said, "You must have hit the wrong Fowler. I was sure with him that night. Hell, we went bowling."

Clark said, "Look, Smith. You might as well stop lying. You weren't anyplace near Concord that night. You've been checked."

"I was——"

"How well did you know Mrs. Ann Durant?" Clark interrupted him.

Adams was watching young Smith. He had never seen a leer before. "A dish," Smith said. "Something, man!"

Then he turned his head slightly. "Hell, Adams ought to know." He laughed lightly. Adams leaned forward, hand upraised, then restrained himself.

"Were you ever in her apartment?" Clark asked.

Smith said, "Well, there was one time when I figure I might have made it, but my old lady——" Then he stopped. "Say, what are you trying to——"

"Were you in her apartment last Sunday night?"

Smith stared at him. "You mean the night that Adams killed her? The hell I was! I was never in the place! That snooty bitch wouldn't—— No! You can't pin that on me! I wasn't anywhere near the place!"

"Where were you?" Clark's voice was cold and clammy. "You weren't in Concord. You weren't in West Fork. Where were you?"

Adams watched young Smith trying to swallow.

Clark said, "You were tried once for rape in the Army and they kicked you out. What about this?"

"No," Smith said. "I was never up in her apartment. I wasn't there Sunday night. I don't know what you're talking about."

"Okay," Clark said. He turned on the ignition and the car started. "We'll go up to Winslow and sweat this out for a couple of hours or a couple of days. We're in no hurry." Adams thought absently that the man could have made a fine career in the theater.

"Wait," young Smith said again. Clark turned off the motor. Adams wondered where he would have gone if Smith hadn't told him to stop. Smith said, "All right. I wasn't in Concord Sunday night. I was over in Hillsboro."

"Good. I suppose some one saw you there?"

Young Smith smiled in a nasty fashion. "I guess so. I was with Mary Lou Gregg."

Even Adams knew the name. Gregg had an electrical shop in town. He was a very respected man.

Clark asked the question very slowly. "You were with Mary Lou Gregg the entire night?"

Smith's smile was full, now. "I sure as hell was. We went to a motel."

Beside him, Adams felt Bill Tate lean forward in the seat and could feel his body tighten. Then Tate relaxed.

Clark hesitated for a moment. "I guess we'll have to prove that. You and I are going across the street to the phone and you're going to tell Mary Lou that you'll pick her up in five minutes and take a short ride. You'll blow the horn at her house and she'll come out. She can tell her parents she'll be back in an hour."

Smith looked at him. "But it's ten o'clock! I can't do that!"

Clark said evenly, "You can do a lot of things, buster. Come on."

They walked across the street and Adams said, "You think he's lying?"

Tate said in a quiet, even voice, "Mary Lou Gregg is my niece. She is sixteen years old. I hope he is lying."

Adams sat back and said nothing. This was a remarkable little town.

In a few minutes Clark and the hulking young Smith came back. Smith's face was strained, now, no hint of laughter in it. They got into the car and Smith said, "Turn left at the next corner." There was a right turn, another left turn, and Smith said, "It's the big house on the far corner." They parked in front of it and Clark tapped the horn twice.

In a few moments the front door opened and a slight figure was framed for a second against the light. The door closed and the girl ran down the walk to the car. Young Smith opened the door and she started to get in, then stopped. Her voice was high. "Henry! What are. . . ?"

From the back seat Tate said, "It's all right, Mary Lou. You can get in."

Her head whipped around. "Uncle Billy! I don't know——"

Tate said, "Get in, Mary Lou." His voice was very gentle. "It's all right, kid. We just want to find out about a few things."

The girl got into the car. Adams was shocked by her youngness. He wished they hadn't done this, but there was no other way. Clark drove slowly down the street.

Tate said, "Mary Lou, we're just trying to find out where Henry was last Sunday night. He says he was with you. He told us that you and he stayed at a motel over in Hillsboro. Is that right?" He sounded like a very tired man.

The girl said nothing for a full minute. She looked at young Smith, then put her face in her hands.

Tate said, "I guess you'd better tell us, Mary Lou."

The girl was sobbing. "He said we were going to a

house party. We had some whisky and coke in the car on the way over, and then when he got to the motel——" She stopped. "Uncle Billy, I didn't mean to . . . If Mother and Pop hear about this . . ."

"They won't," Tate said. "We just want to know if Henry was with you all night."

The answer was long in coming. It was whispered. "Yes, Uncle Billy."

There was silence in the car, then Clark said, "I think we'd better check it."

Tate said, "Okay. Take the next right turn and go out the Hillsboro road."

It was an almost silent ride. Once young Smith said, "I don't know why you're going to all this mess just to——"

Clark told him, "Keep your mouth shut."

He did.

Adams could think of nothing to say, so he said nothing. It took them half an hour to drive to Hillsboro, and Smith pointed out the motel. Clark and young Smith got out of the car and Adams followed them feeling that he ought to leave Tate and the young girl alone.

In the motel office a stout man got up from behind a desk. His smile was oily. "Yes, gents?"

Clark pointed to Smith. "Do you recognize him? Do you remember if he was here last Sunday night?"

The man looked at Smith. "He's been here, all right. Sunday? I forget one day from the other. Who are you?"

Clark opened a wallet and there was a flash of metal. Adams didn't see the badge but it must have been impressive. The man said, "All right. All right." He consulted a ledger. In a moment he looked up, beaming. "Yessir, he was here last Sunday. With his wife. Mr. and Mrs. Jones."

Clark said, "For God's sake! Jones!"

They went out. Young Smith wore a broad smile. "You see, Adams? While you were with that Durant broad, I was——"

Adams hit him fast, a left hook low in the belly and a right hand chopping as Smith's head came down. The big body rolled in the snow. Adams stood over him, saw that he was conscious. He said, "You're a big miserable son of a bitch. Walk home. And when you get home pack your clothes and leave West Fork or Bill Tate will be after you with a gun. You're lucky."

He and Clark walked to the car in silence. He saw Smith sit up, looking at the car as it drove away.

When they neared the Gregg house Tate broke the silence. "No one is going to hear about this, Mary Lou. I'm sorry it happened. It's really none of our business, but the circumstances were confusing." The girl was crying silently. "If anyone in the house says anything you can tell them you had an argument with Henry."

The girl opened the door and went up the walk, her head low.

Adams said, "Willy, I'm sorry."

Tate said, "It's all right. It's just that she's so young. Hell, it seems like last week when I was giving her pennies for candy. I'm sorry for her it was that slob."

They drove up the hill to the hotel. Adams said, "I think we could all stand a drink. Come on in."

Tate shook his head. "Some other time, John."

Clark looked at Adams. "I guess we'd better be getting along."

"Keep in touch," Adams said. "Drop by." He watched the car start the trip back to town, then went into the hotel.

It was a busy night. He was greeted in a quiet fashion by all the people he knew, introduced to their friends. He found in nearly everyone a reserve tinged with a bit of morbidity. He told Helen, "I feel as if I ought to be in Madame Tussaud's. One guy even took a picture of me."

"What went on this evening?" she wanted to know.

He told her, and she said, "Poor kid. You sure put her into a mess."

"The idea was that Smith might have conned her into giving him an alibi. We had to make sure. I was sorry for the girl but I am not as concerned about the morals of the young as I am about the health of the Adams neck."

"Don't say that, even in joking."

And Adams looked at her. "I'm definitely not joking."

Chapter 21

SATURDAY WAS A BUSY TIME. The house was filled to overflowing and the bar so crowded Adams wondered if any of this bunch had bothered to bring skis. "If this keeps up," he told Helen, "I'll be one of the richest men ever to be executed in this state."

Helen paled but she said, "Maybe you ought to call the place Ghoul House."

Gordon came back from Bald Mountain late in the afternoon. "What's new in the annals of crime?"

"Adams has grown morbid," Helen said. "Instead of having a Bible in each room he's going to distribute copies of *Hangman's House*."

"Our lawyers will be up Monday," Gordon said. "Maybe we'll get something done."

"I have a lawyer," Adams told him. "What I need is a nice fat juicy murderer." He happened to be looking at the door and saw Mayo come in. He went over and the lieutenant said,

"Talk to you?"

"Always a pleasure." Adams led the way into his small apartment and closed the door. "What's on your mind, Lieutenant?"

"I understand you and a couple of people were talking to young Smith last night."

"Smith? I seem to recall having heard the name somewhere."

Mayo looked at him and said nothing.

"All right," Adams said. "I talked to Smith."

"You and someone representing himself as an officer."

Adams shook his head. "What Smith was told and what he chose to believe are a couple of different things. No one represented himself as the law."

"You're edging it close, Adams. You can get yourself in trouble and you already have just about as much of that as one man can handle. These private hawkshaws get themselves jammed up once in a while."

"That punk was scared. He inferred what was never said."

Mayo considered that for a moment. "All right, so you talked to Smith. What did he have to say?"

Adams thought about the girl. "Nothing."

"He had nothing to say, yet you knocked him down outside a motel in Hillsboro last night."

"I did? Smith?"

"Stop trying to be cute, Adams. What did you expect to find out from him?"

Adams shrugged. "I found out just enough to convince me he had nothing to do with Mrs. Durant's death."

Mayo's eyebrows went up. "You suspected him?"

"In the dandy little fix I'm in I suspect you, Lieutenant."

Mayo looked at him and nodded. Then he said, "You might be interested to know that Smith left town on the late train."

"Well, think of that!"

"All right. You were foolish, but you did us a favor. He's been a lot of trouble and we're glad to get rid of him."

"If I can ever be of service to you, Lieutenant . . ."

"Don't try. My job is tough enough as it is. You amateurs really foul things up."

Adams felt his mouth tighten. "The professionals aren't performing in a fashion that would incline me to throw my hat in the air. I'm out on a limb, and any way I can get off it is the best way for me. Don't think for a moment I won't stick my nose into any part of this pie it can reach."

"You've got a point, but don't press it too hard. You'll do more harm than good."

"What particular harm could I do?"

Mayo moved toward the door. "Go easy, Adams."

"Sure. I'll mind my manners and die like a little gentleman."

"Maybe you'll have to do that," Mayo said. He left.

Sunday was a beautiful day and everyone deserted the bar and fled to the hill. Adams told Helen, "Take a day off. You're looking tired. Go over to Bald Mountain with Gordon and relax."

She said, "Boss, it's all right with me."

The day went slowly but easily. In the afternoon people started drifting back to attend to their drinking, and in the early evening the check-outs kept Adams reasonably busy. It was full dark when Helen and Gordon returned and Adams went with them into the bar for a drink.

Helen said, "Guess who we saw. We stopped at Pepper's for a drink."

"I like that. Wasting your money with the opposition. Okay, whom did you see?"

"A certain Miss Mary Knowles. Very charming." Helen looked at Gordon and grinned.

Gordon coughed. "It was some years ago. I was merely interested in the girl's career."

"And that's why she calls you 'Gordiebug'?"

"I was more or less an . . . uncle to her, is all."

Helen's eyes widened. "I've heard of families like that, but I didn't think——"

Adams said, "Okay. So you met her. So what?"

Helen shrugged. "Nothing. Just about the most attractive little old niece anyone could have. But too old to be Gordon's niece, if you get what I mean."

"The charming Mr. Durant with her?"

Helen shook her head. "She had a drink with us, but he wasn't discussed."

Adams was interested. "What is she like?"

"Lovely," Helen said, and reached over and pinned an imaginary medal on Gordon, who inclined his head in a bow of acceptance. "Sharp. Seemed like a nice person."

"She is," Gordon said.

"What is she doing with a monkey like Durant?"

Helen shrugged. "I understand he is, or was, very attractive. And a lot of money doesn't frighten some girls."

Adams was silent for a moment. "You know, I think I'd like to talk to Miss Knowles."

"She's really not much of a conversationalist," Gordon said. "More the active type."

Helen said, "Phil Gordon!"

"Disregarding your elemental minds," Adams said, "Miss Knowles might know an interesting fact or two."

"She has already said Durant was with her that night," Gordon pointed out.

"I wonder just how thoroughly she was questioned. As to time, and things like that. Maybe if I talked to her, girl to girl, she might remember something important."

"There's little chance of you talking with her girl to girl," Helen said. 'Wait until you see her."

"And no Durant," Adams mused.

"She's been drinking," Gordon said. "If she continues at her present pace she won't be doing much talking in another hour or so, if my memory serves me."

"It might just possibly be the right time to see her."

Helen's face reflected doubt. Gordon said, "You'd be

wasting your time, Johnny. If she told the police she was with Durant she's not going to tell you any different. She's really a nice person, and as Helen said, she is no fool."

"I'd like to talk to her," Adams said stubbornly. "I couldn't possibly do any harm."

"You've got Durant on your mind merely because he's unpleasant," Helen said. "You seem to have forgotten about Joe Cooley."

"He's too nice a guy."

"I'm sure that Jack the Ripper's mother loved him. What has *nice* got to do with it? When people get very emotional they change the pattern. A combination of drunkenness and jealousy can easily result in murder."

"He wasn't that involved," Adams said.

"I'd say that standing around in the cold, night after night, is being slightly involved. You don't do this just out of curiosity. Just because Durant was reasonably angry that his ex-wife had been killed and came over here and hit you is no excuse for——"

Adams got up. "Okay. But I see I have some work to do."

He attended to guests for another two hours, but Mary Knowles was on his mind. The simple statement to police that Durant had spent the night with her was quite a commitment, he allowed, but the hours before dawn are frequently hazy periods to a person who, as Gordon had intimated, was not a stranger to the bottle.

At ten o'clock he checked the last departure, Lenny Knight and his wife. Lenny, an old friend, said, "Johnny, if there's anything I can do to help with this mess, I——"

Adams said, "Thanks, Lenny. It'll work out somehow," and thought with gratitude of the many people who had offered their assistance.

He called Pepper's Inn, then, and asked for Mr. Durant. He was told that Durant had checked out the day before. Then he called Pine Lodge and asked for Miss Knowles. He hung up as the operator was ringing the room.

Gordon was still in the bar. Adams said to him, "Would this Knowles girl be up here without Durant?"

Gordon considered for only a moment. "Why not? She

loves to ski and has the day off. And she's good. I taught her," he added modestly.

Adams said, "I'm going to run over and have a talk with her."

Gordon glanced at his watch. "If I remember correctly, and I believe I do, you're about two hours late, from the way she was drinking late this afternoon."

"We'll give it a try," Adams told him. He put on a heavy coat and went out to his car.

On the ride to Bald Mountain he asked himself what he expected to discover. The woman would say that Durant had been with her that night, or she might tell Adams simply to go climb a convenient tree. There was actually very little point to the trip, since the interview would be completely without authority. But he felt he had to talk to the woman. Anything was better than just sitting around hoping that something would turn up.

There were still plenty of people at Pine Lodge, and Adams went into the bar and had a drink. He looked around but could see no one who might conceivably be Mary Knowles. There was no evidence of Durant. He finished his drink and went out into the lobby. There was a bellboy standing near the entrance. Adams showed him a five-dollar bill. "What room is Miss Knowles in?"

The man grinned and took the bill. "Number 245. But listen——"

Adams supplied the additional five he had in his other hand. "Let's just say no more about it."

The man shrugged and said, "Okay, Mac. Have it your way."

Adams waited for a moment, and when a group of three women and a man started up the stairs he quietly joined him. Number 245 was not difficult to find. The hallway was empty when Adams knocked on the door. He heard the sound of someone moving inside the room, then the door opened.

Durant stood there. His nose was taped and there was a strip of adhesive along his lower lip. He had obviously been doing a lot of drinking. He said. "Adams. Well. What do you want?"

"I want to see Miss Knowles." Adams couldn't have been more surprised.

"Fine. And what do you want to see Miss Knowles about?"

"I thought I might be lucky enough to get her autograph. I'm a great fan of Miss Knowles's."

"Very smart, aren't you, Adams. Autograph. It couldn't be that you'd like to get into bed with her the way you do with some of my women?"

"You can never tell," Adams said.

Durant opened the door wide. "Come in. Come in, Adams. I've always wanted to know what you were like."

Adams couldn't see that he had anything to lose. He went in and Durant closed the door. The room was a large sitting room, and a door evidently connected with a bedroom. Suites. A bit of swank his own place could not boast.

There was a bottle and glasses on the table. Durant gestured toward them. "Help yourself. Hospitality is the watchword. Especially toward someone with whom I have such common interests."

Adams said, "Thanks, but I've had some. About Miss Knowles."

"Miss Knowles," Durant said, "is dead drunk and sound asleep." He laughed shortly. "Has a fine habit of being dead drunk and sound asleep. She is not available for any autographing this evening."

Adams took a stab. "She couldn't just have been dead drunk and sound asleep the night you killed Ann?"

Durant stared at him, then smiled coldly. "The police asked questions, Adams. Expertly. What do you expect to find that they couldn't?"

"It was just an old question I had hanging around," Adams said. "I thought I'd give it a workout." He was not sure, but he thought he had detected something very much like fear in Durant's eyes for a moment. He sat down and Durant poured himself a heavy drink from the bottle.

Adams said, "Why did you kill her, Durant? She wasn't doing anything to you."

Durant turned to him slowly, smiling. "I, Adams? My good fellow, just at the precise moment you were strangling my ex-wife, I was enjoying the charms of Miss Knowles. She admitted her indiscretion to the police. A pity that a matter of such privacy had to be aired, but she's a courageous girl and saved me a great deal of embarrassment."

Adams continued, almost hopelessly. "Ann was through

with you, entirely out of your life. She had no feeling for you left, hadn't even seen you for a long while. Why did you do it, Durant?"

Durant drank. "You're foolish, Adams. What do you think you're doing? That tramp in the next room cleared me completely."

Adams got up. It was useless. He said, "No wonder Ann despised you. You're a real louse, Durant."

He was shocked when Durant flung his glass across the room. When the man got to his feet and staggered. "*She* despised *me?* That bitch? That cold, smug bitch? She sickened me with her righteousness! Oh, she was smiling and charming to the rest of the world. Friends? Everyone was her friend. Everyone found her delightful and tender and generous and kind. They didn't know her the way I did. Remote, removed. Selfish and grasping and bitter."

Adams watched him as he walked to the table and red a drink into a glass, then drained it. The tirade tinued.

She was cold and conniving. She was after one thing, money. Oh, she was human at first, until she had me snagged. Then she was a stick, a piece of ice. I ght as well have been her dog." He looked directly at Adams for the first time. "And then I found out that she'd taken up with you. *I* wasn't good enough for her, but she'd sleep with some nothing like you! Can you imagine it?"

Adams regarded with something like awe the towering egotism of the man.

"And you hadn't been the first. Don't flatter yourself about that. But the others had been acceptable. A Polish count. An English yachtsman with a title. Nothing like you, Adams. You were the last straw."

Sick, Adams thought. *God, how sick.*

Durant tasted his drink. "Of course I killed her." He gestured with his head toward the next room. "Give her a quart of whisky and a few sleeping pills and the world is gone for her. I thought you'd never leave that night, Adams. And there was some other fool standing across the street in the cold for hours. What sort of establishment was she running?" Then the face went cold. "She was very surprised to see me. Very surprised."

Adams felt exhausted. He sank into a chair, but the voice pulled him to his feet.

"Don't mind me. I'm just the tramp in the other room."

The woman was in the doorway separating the two rooms. She was tall and red-haired and under the sheer nightgown her body was beautiful. Her face was pale and drawn and she leaned with one hand against the door frame.

"Just a quart and a few pills," she said. "Brother, what a patsy is little old Mary."

Durant glared at her. "Shut your mouth! You didn't hear a thing!"

Her mouth was ugly. "Did I not, as we so often say on the stage. Brother, did I not!"

"You got it all?" Adams asked.

She regarded him almost with disinterest. "So he slept with me that night, and me out like a light. I woke up once and missed him but I thought he might have gone to the john and I was too dead to care. It would have been a hell of a thing for me if it had come out in the papers, but he was in a jam and a mink coat here and a mink coat there buy a guy a little loyalty. So I said all right, he was with me. And I honestly thought he was."

Durant said, "I was. You know that."

The woman shook her head slowly. "No, Sidney darling. There was a time that night when you were not with your tramp. The papers will murder me on this but I hate the thought of jails."

She turned to go into the other room and Durant said, "Who'll believe that slut?"

"Somebody will," Adams said. "Don't worry about that." He had never been so tired in his life.

There was a knock on the door and Durant moved toward it. Adams shoved him aside and opened the door. Mayo came into the room. He said, "Hope I'm not disturbing you? Didn't break up a gin game?"

"It's nice to see you," Adams told him.

"I stopped by your place and your wife told me you were over here. I thought I'd look in."

"There's a young lady in the next room who might like to say a few well-chosen words to you."

"I guess I've heard them," Mayo said.

"You've heard them?"

"The conversation of the last half hour is on a tape

recorder in the next room. This room was wired two days ago."

"Think of that," Adams said. He looked at Durant. The man was standing stiffly erect.

Durant said, "You can't use that as evidence."

"Oh, I think it will hold up," Mayo said. "Especially with the corroboration of Miss Knowles." He looked at Adams. "You're a little impatient, Adams. We're not completely incompetent. We discovered that Durant did leave here for a couple of hours that morning, but for all we knew he might have gone for a drive. His room at Pepper's was bugged for a few days, and when this reservation was made we just moved over. We thought it might be interesting to hear what they said to each other."

"It was very interesting," Adams said.

"Well, you sparked it. I must give you credit for that. Next time you get a ticket for speeding try to get in touch with me. I'll see what I can do."

Adams said, "Thanks." He looked once more at Durant. There was no emotion evident on the man's face. Adams said, "Well, take care of things."

Mayo said, "We'll try. See you soon."

Down in the bar Adams sat at a table and tasted his big drink. He felt as if he had just been guided out of a cave where he had been wandering helplessly for days. He thought of Durant with horror and then of Cooley with relief. It was nice to know that you were right once in a while. He got up and went to a phone booth in a corner and called the hotel. Helen answered and he said, "It's all wrapped up. It was Durant, of course. I'll explain it all later."

There was a pause, then Helen said, "Did you love her, Johnny? Ann Durant?"

Adams thought about it, examined his emotions. Regret was there. Regret at the loss of so much warmth and beauty. Sorrow. Deep sorrow at the loss of a dear friend. There was no despair. He said, "Yes."

Helen was slow in asking. "In the way you loved me? In the way we loved?"

His mind walked back through the years. It was an easy answer. It was not a betrayal. He said, "No. Not that way."

Helen said, "All right." Just that. She hung up.

He finished his drink and went out through the lobby. The bellhop who had taken his ten said, "Everything all right, sir? I tried to tell you there was someone up there, but you wouldn't listen. I was afraid there might be some trouble."

"Everything was fine," Adams told him. "Nothing you could really call trouble." He went out to his car.